The Abuse

The Abuse

Ulla Bolinder

Translated from the Swedish by
Eric Swanson
in collaboration with the author

Originally published in Sweden as *Övergreppet*
by Anamma 1997 and BoD 2019
© Ulla Bolinder 1997, 2019
English Translation © Eric Swanson 2020
Cover: Ulla Bolinder
Cover photos: Pixabay
Publisher: BoD – Books on Demand, Stockholm, Sweden
Print: BoD – Books on Demand, Norderstedt, Germany
ISBN: 978-91-7969-825-6

Rape has its inner, private meaning for every victim.

PART ONE

1992

Coming out on the street, out into the light on the street
Close to losing balance, take support against the house
wall
Do not see, do not know
Close my eyes
Feel a hand on my arm, a hand that seizes me by the arm
What has happened to you, then
happened to you
It goes around in my head, my legs almost give way
under me
must not faint, must not fall
The hand grips harder
do not fall
Standing against the wall, standing pressed against the
wall
Do you need help
Open my eyes, see his face
eyes, nose, mouth
Has anyone been unpleasant to you
unpleasant
My throat stings, my tongue feels stiff
must go home, must get my bag and go home, must go
back and fetch my bag
Sway, catch hold of
Take it easy, I'm holding you, it will be all right

The lamp on the wall, the clothes on the ground, scattered on the ground, thrown on the gravel, the torn gravel, the tracks in the gravel

Walking in the pale light on the street, walking beside him on the pavement, on the cold pavement
Feeling his arm around my back, his thigh against my hip, his leg against my thigh
he helps me
My knees below the edge of the long cardigan, my knees and feet mechanically moving forward along the sidewalk, my feet in dirty ankle socks against the paving stones, hard and cold stone under my feet, the wind cooling between my legs
It cuts and burns for every step, burns for every step, cuts and burns
must come along, must go with him into

Sitting on a chair with my hands on my knee, sitting tense and still with my legs close together
It smells of smoke and perfume, the air stands still, rustling of clothes, scraping of shoes, murmuring of voices, clattering of porcelain
inside the restaurant people are sitting and eating as if nothing has happened
Soon the police will be here
the police

What has happened here, then
Looking at his hand, looking at his hand next to his

uniform trousers, gaze at his — stare straight at his
See the trouser leg, the holster, the shoulder belt
Hear his voice, the voices, the voice
Has someone been nasty to you
nasty
My throat feels thick, my head is empty
must sit silent and still, silent and empty in the dark,
must not give in, must not let it out, must not let it
Yes, now you will soon come with us here
the police, must go with the police

Getting into the police car, into the dark in the back seat
of the police car
cannot manage, must lie down, must rest
No, now you can't
Now you must
must sit up
The car slides quietly away across the asphalt, shadows
and lights in front of my eyes, crackling voices in the
radio, the call signal tones in the radio
must come along

Sitting on the chair with my cardigan pulled down as far
as possible
My back and throat are aching, it aches and burns
between my legs
not seriously injured
The lamp lights up the tabletop, the chair feels warm
underneath my body, warm and sticky under my body
have no briefs under my cardigan, is he thinking of that,

can he resist thinking of that
Tense my body, make my body numb
may not relax, may not feel, must tell what happened,
must remember how it happened, must take it easy, must
have a cigarette and calm down, smoke and calm down

Holding the cigarette between my fingers, there are red
stains on my fingers, reddish brown stains on my fingers, dried blood on my fingers
where does it come from, must go and wash it away
No, now you can't
First you must

Standing naked on the floor under the lamp
my face is dirty, my face smells bad
Have you got something inserted into

It stings and burns between my legs, stings and burns
will soon pass
Wash hands and face
do not become clean
The door is unlocked, anyone can come in
nobody comes in
My body is tense, my legs are trembling
must go out now, must continue, must manage, must
help

Face after face
He may not be included
is not included

Sitting at the table with the door closed, alone with him with the door closed
man, policeman, detective inspector, police officer
Could you please give an account of the course of events as accurately as possible
cannot give an account
Questions and answers, questions and answers
unable to be with it, haven't put up with it yet, cannot follow

His hands on the steering wheel, streetlights gliding in over his thighs, down over his thighs, down between his parted legs
alone in the car with
It is cold, my feet are cold, a ribbed rubber mat under my feet
no briefs under my cardigan
Controlling that the buttoning of my cardigan does not gape open
Darkness and light, no traffic, streetlights on the empty asphalt

When I came home Bernt was awake. The movie had ended before half past ten, but I didn't come home until after three. I hadn't called him either, because I thought he was sleeping and that it was unnecessary to waken him. But he was up.

I hurried into the bathroom, and there I quickly put on a pair of already used briefs that I dug out of the laundry basket. I had to make an effort not to lock the door behind me. The ankle socks I threw into the refuse pail. Then I peed, washed my hands and face, and went out to Bernt.

He had been sitting and smoking at the kitchen table, because the light was on and the ashtray was full of butts. He had also been drinking a little, but not so much that he was drunk.

"What the hell have you been up to?" he said, sounding like he thought I had been out with another guy. I didn't want to talk with him when he sounded that suspicious and on his guard. But I had to tell him what had happened.

He went back to the table and sat down and lighted a cigarette, and I saw that he was upset. His face was like a stiff mask, and his voice was hard and cold, as it often is when he is either angry or feels uncertain and afraid.

– *Come out with it now! Where have you been?*
  – *I have been with the police.*
  – *With the police?*
  – *Yes, something happened after the movie.*
  – *What kind of thing?*
  – *It was just a guy who became a bit intrusive.*
  – *What fucking guy?*
  – *One who turned up when I was on my way to the bus.*
  – *And what did he do?*

He had probably become worried when I hadn't come home the time I was expected to. But I felt almost… *elated* and said that a guy had come and started arguing with me – and he could easily understand in what way, when he saw that I didn't have all my clothes on.

He asked what had happened to the clothes.

"They were left there," I said. "The police took care of them later."

"But they didn't get hold of the guy?"

And I didn't know that, but if that had been the case, I assumed the police would have told me, so I said he had escaped. Then he said that he would go out and try to find him. I thought he was ridiculous, because how could he find him after so long? By then he had had plenty of time to disappear.

And what would he have done if he had got hold of him? Beaten him up? But he would never had succeeded in that, because that guy was much bigger and stronger than him. And he didn't care about what had happened to me, so it was just ridiculous of him to talk like that.

And he didn't go. I hadn't believed he would either. He stayed at the kitchen table and smoked and didn't say anything more.

When I had undressed in the bathroom and saw all the marks on my body, I almost got a shock. I had never seen such big and dark bruises before. I hurried to lock the door so that Bernt couldn't come in and see me. I barely dared to look myself. It looked like I had been in an accident.

In the shower I gently soaped myself, and it stung everywhere, but I couldn't let the water run for too long, because it was in the middle of the night. I thought I could shower one more time after I had slept.

Bernt had gone to bed, but he was still awake when I came into the bedroom. I had put on a nightgown with long sleeves, and I went quickly to bed and turned off the lamp so that he wouldn't see the marks. I didn't want him to get the wrong impression and maybe believe that it had been worse than it was. After all, it doesn't take much to get a bruise.

It didn't feel well to lie so close to him and not

know what he was thinking or what he could do. I was afraid he would touch me, against both his and my will. But he didn't do anything, and at last I heard that he was asleep.

I don't want to be seen like this. The marks on my body are not visible, but the one on my face I can't hide, nor the bruises on my arms. Yes, if I have long-sleeved sweaters on, and I mostly have now in the autumn, so it will probably work. I don't want people to start wondering and asking what has happened to me. If it hadn't been necessary, I wouldn't have told Bernt about it either.

It's in the newspaper today. I have clipped it out and intend to save it. I don't know if Bernt has read it. I hope he missed it, because I think it's none of his business.

ATTEMPTED RAPE. A woman in her twenties, resident in Uppsala, was molested late on Friday evening by an attempted rape in central Uppsala. She was walking on Vaksalagatan when suddenly a man turned up behind her and forced her into the back yard of Vaksalagatan 25. The perpetrator was wearing a dark windcheater and is described as being 20 to 25 years old as well as power-fully built. He was at midnight still at large.

My whole body hurts. It feels like pain after train-ing. And the bruises are sore. But otherwise there isn't anything.

At the police station there was a policeman who asked me if I had experienced similar things before, because I was taking it so easy. But everyone want-ed me to tell what had happened as quickly as pos-sible, and then I couldn't care about my feelings at the same time.

Earlier, when I was sitting in the police car, I thought I could relax a little. It was as if I were stunned, and it felt like I couldn't stay up. At first, I thought that the police officer beside me perhaps would hold me or give me a blanket to wrap myself up in, but he didn't. He did nothing at all. Not until I leaned my upper body to the side and tried to lay down on the seat and pulled my legs up, he did react.

"No, now you can't lie down, now you must try to give us a description of him," he said.

After that, I didn't try again.

The police officers might have thought that I had agreed to it in the beginning but regretted it later, because I seemed so composed. That wasn't the case, but it was my own fault that it happened. I hadn't needed to be there.

I don't know why I go out like that sometimes, without Bernt. I don't know what the point is, other than I want to be a little by myself for a while. Now it feels like what happened is the punishment for me going out, and that I only have myself to blame. Because I walked there and wished the evening wouldn't end. That's why I didn't feel as negative as I should have done, when that guy started walking beside me. I looked at him to see if he were handsome or not and tried to feel if I liked his looks. If I had been completely uninterested, I wouldn't have done so.

But he was rather ugly and didn't feel nice, so I lost interest immediately. And he might have noticed that. Perhaps that's why he got angry and grabbed me when I turned away. Anyway, I don't think he had decided in advance that he would stand there waiting for a suitable victim to turn up. If I had just answered what time it was and hadn't sized him up like I did, he perhaps wouldn't have done more. Or if I hadn't answered at all. But that could also have made him angry. And it seems so impolite to not answer when a person comes and asks for information.

"Here comes someone who's walked into a door," Egon said when I came to work and he saw the bruise on my cheek. I know what people mean by saying so, but I didn't correct him. I didn't even bother to lie to him. He is just a boring old man who I don't need to pay any attention to.

"Sure," I said and walked away.

Viola must also have seen the bruise, but she didn't say anything.

I was able to work even though I was tense. I did just as I usually do. Sometimes I got stuck and sat staring straight ahead without thinking. When it felt like I was about to burst I took a cigarette or went to the toilet and washed myself. Once I went into Göran's room and closed the door. I just stood there and didn't know what to do. I thought that if he came and found me, I could have let it out and got help. But he wasn't there.

In the evening, the police called and asked me to come to the police station the next day and fetch my clothes. It was Bernt who answered, and when he said I was wanted on the phone, he looked angry and weird again, as if it is very embarrassing and unpleasant for him that I have been involved with the police, and that I should be ashamed and apologize to him for that.

At the police station, I got to meet the same policeman as last time. We sat in his office, and he talked about the weather and said that the evening darkness comes earlier and earlier in the afternoons now, and that it can feel a bit depressing that the daylight has disappeared when it's time to go home from work.

I said almost nothing, because I couldn't bear to be polite, and I couldn't relax, though that's probably what he was trying to get me to do by talking about other things like that. I thought it was because of me he couldn't go home before it had become dark, and I felt guilty.

The police had done a crime scene investigation and found a beer can and a shoeprint inside the yard, he said. I was surprised when he told me, because I didn't think that crimes, where no one has been seriously injured, were investigated so carefully. Fingerprints and footprints, I thought were only looked for in serious crimes.

After a while he took out a bag with my clothes and put it on the desk. It was my coat, long trousers and shoes. My briefs lay in a transparent plastic bag which he held up.

"Well, these, I suppose, are just to be thrown

away?" he said and dropped the bag into the waste-paper basket.

Then he began to interrogate me. He had to ask questions the whole time to help me get through it.

– And what happened after that?

– He started walking beside me.

– What did you think then? How did you perceive his intentions?

– I thought he was going the same direction as me. But then I thought that…

– Yes?

– That he was looking for company.

– And how did you react to that?

– Negatively.

– You weren't interested?

– No.

As I answered, he repeated it and recorded it on a tape.

Sometimes it became a bit painful. When I was going to say that I suggested I could masturbate the guy, I didn't know if I should say masturbate or jack off, but I chose jack off, and when he recorded it he said: "With the hope that the man would leave her alone if he got an ejaculation, she offered to masturbate him."

Then he turned off the tape recorder and said:

"And then you jacked him off?"

Isn't it called masturbate? I thought. I was close

to saying it out loud. At the same time, I should have smiled a little archly at him, I felt. I don't know what got into me. Because what kind of an impression would that have made, if I had begun to joke about sex in that situation? From that he could have believed that I did the same when it happened.

It was fortunate that I managed to control myself. But I was close to laughing because he seemed to believe that I wouldn't understand if he said masturbate. I mostly say masturbate, but to that guy I said jack off, and that's why I also used that word when I was interrogated.

– Use whatever words you want. If it's easier for you to use slang expressions, just do that, and if you think it's easier to use more strict words, do that. The main thing is that I get to know exactly what he did to you. Do you understand?

That I felt like joking was perhaps because I wanted to relieve the atmosphere a little, so that the policeman who questioned me would understand that he didn't have to take it so seriously.

When I came home, Bernt asked me how it had turned out.

"What did the cop say, then? Had they caught the bastard?"

"No, and I don't think they will either," I said.

"No, and that's just as well, perhaps?"

It seems like he thinks I am glad that the police haven't found him. As if I actually hope that he gets away. But why should I hope that?

Bernt has been so weird since it happened, and I don't know what to do to get him back to normal again. He tends to be kind, but now he isn't any longer. He seems suspicious and angry, like he believes I agreed to it, or that I didn't defend myself as much as I should have done, or that it was I who attracted him to me.

Today it's in the newspaper again. I was surprised when I saw it, because I thought the police didn't think what happened was particularly important. I was hoping that Bernt hadn't read it before I clipped it out, but he had.

THE POLICE WANT HELP TO FIND A RAPIST. Last Friday at about 10.30 p.m., a 22-year-old woman was subjected to a rape attempt in central Uppsala. On Vaksalagatan south of Storgatan the woman was molested by a man 20 to 25 years old. At gunpoint he forced the woman into the yard of Vaksalagatan 25. However, the woman succeeded in getting loose and running away before the rape was completed. The man, still at large, was about 180 cm tall, had a powerful build, a broad face as well as short-cropped, light hair. The criminal police are eager to come in contact with people who were observed passing the place in question. Those who have information about the case are encouraged to contact the criminal police in Uppsala.

"Oh really, it was at gunpoint?" he said and looked

like he often does when he finds things unpleasant. His face becomes stiff and expressionless, as if he tries to hide what he is feeling behind an empty mask. And then he said that I obviously had had plenty of time to study "the bastard", because I remembered his appearance so well.

And I had, but not in the way he meant. I didn't think so carefully about it before I was to describe him to the police. I had to do that already in the police car, before we went to the station, so that the police message could be sent out immediately to other policemen who would keep a lookout for him. But by then he had already had time to disappear. Because so stupid, that he continued to walk around in town afterwards, I don't think he was.

– I know it can be hard, but you must give us as many details as possible about his appearance so that we can notify the radio patrol cars. You must provide us with both a description of him, and all other information that could help us to catch him.

– Yes.

– Can you describe to me what he looked like?

– Yes, he was rather tall…

– About how tall?

– I don't know. I'm so bad at…

– Compare with your own height. Was he a head taller than you?

– Yes, approximately.

– And how tall are you?

– One and sixty-five.

– I see… And what kind of bodily constitution did he have?

– He was powerfully built.

– Big and muscular or more ordinarily powerful?

– More ordinarily.

– What colour was his hair then?

– It was light.

– Long or short?

– Short.

– Crew cut?

– No, short on the sides and longer on top.

– And his face? Can you describe his face?

– Yes, it was broad. Square, so to say. And his eyes were light. I don't know which colour, but they weren't brown anyway.

– Okay. Anything else?

– I don't know… Well, there was something about his nose.

– Yes?

– It was flattened.

– In what way?

– Pressed in against his face, so to say.

– Did he have a so-called boxer nose? Is that what you mean?

– Yes.

– I see… And how old could he be?

– Twenty, twenty-five perhaps…

– How was he dressed then? Did you think of that?

– Yes, he had a dark blue jacket and jeans.

– What kind of jacket?

– A short one, with a zipper in front and elastic at the bottom.

– A so-called windcheater?

– Yes. And on his feet, he had white gym shoes.

– Let's see then… He was strongly built, about a hundred and eighty centimetres tall, had light, short-cropped hair and was dressed in a dark blue jacket, jeans, and white gym shoes. Is that a correct summary?

– Yes.

– Then we'll send it out. Is there anything else you remember about his appearance? He had no scars, tattoos, or other special identification marks?

– No, just that with the nose.

– No accent?

– No.

– And you didn't find out what his name was? He didn't say anything that revealed his identity?

– No.

– Then I only have one more question, and that is if you think you would recognize him if you got to see him again.

– Yes, I think so.

– That's good. Let's go then.

Today Göran came back to work. He has been off, and I haven't met him since it happened. As soon as he saw me, he asked how I had got the bruise on my face. I said that I had got it from a corner of a book that had fallen from a shelf, because that's what I had decided to say if I would get the question. But I don't think he believed me. I think he suspects that it was Bernt who had hit me.

I know I am a coward who dares not tell the truth, but if Viola, for instance, would find out what has happened, she would want to know what I feel and perhaps start feeling sorry for me, and I couldn't stand that. She would pretend to understand and play frightened and compassionate because she thinks that's the way one *should* react. At the same time, she would revel in it and be horrified at all the terrible rapists who roam about on the streets. I don't know why I think so.

And she would tell Egon, who could probably do the same thing himself. No, but he is disgusting. Comes and leans over you when you are sitting at the table, or happens to brush against you when you go by, or places himself near you when there are things he wants to show. If he found out that a guy has tried to rape me, he would perhaps be even more slimy.

Viola heard what Göran and I talked about and said that she thought I looked tired. And I have had a little difficulty sleeping lately. I lie and think about everything so I can't relax, and if I manage to fall asleep, I get glimpses of pictures and words in my head, so I wake up again. Sometimes I have had nightmares.

I also smoke more. I am probably up to a pack a day now. It's almost disgusting, but I do it anyway.

That guy smoked too. I forgot to tell the police about that. When he covered my mouth, I felt that it smelled of nicotine on his fingers. But probably it doesn't matter that he smoked, because almost everyone does.

Sometimes it feels like I would like to curl up and hide under a thick quilt and just lie there in the warmth and darkness and not have to care about how everything is.

But it's impossible. I am never alone. When I was lying on our bed, Bernt came and stretched beside me and tried to hold me. He wanted to have sex with me, but I withdrew, because he wasn't quite sober, and I don't like to do it when he has been drinking.

Then he rolled aside and started to masturbate instead. He decided to take the thing in his own hands and draw the conclusion himself. I almost got a shock, because I had never seen him do that before, and I didn't want to watch. I turned away, and at first, I thought he would let me be, but after a while he said he wanted me to help.

"Come on now and show me what you did with that prick in town," he said. "Because that one you surely haven't forgotten? No, just as I thought! What size was that one then? You haven't told me. And not what you did with it either."

How can he talk like that when he doesn't know what happened? Why does he believe I held it? He can't know what I did.

Then I saw that he had a porno magazine open beside him, and I haven't seen him with that kind of magazine before either. I didn't know he is using pornography. And even if I hadn't said that I didn't want to – and I wanted it even less then, when I had seen him lie and get aroused with pictures – I didn't resist when he took off my clothes and raised himself up on top of me. He has let me be the whole time since it happened, and I can't expect him to be without it forever.

But he was so weird. It felt like he was angry and wanted to punish me. He pushed and groaned and said:

"Is this how the bull did it? Is this how he fucked you?"

Why does he talk like that when he knows I got away? Or does he think I lied to the police?

And he saw almost all the bruises. At first, I was ashamed, but then I thought it was just as well, because now he must believe that I offered resistance. He didn't say anything, but I felt that he found it unpleasant.

PART TWO

I feel tense and have difficulty relaxing. Some evenings I take a glass of wine before I go to bed so that I can fall asleep easier. I know I must not make it a habit, but I get so tired during the days if I can't sleep at night, and I would rather not feel unfocused at work. Sometimes Bernt accompanies me and takes a glass too, but actually I don't want him to, because it isn't because I wish to be together with him that I drink, but to be able to fall asleep. He and I have nothing to talk about anyway.

That guy had also been drinking. His breath smelled of alcohol, and in his jacket pocket he had a pocket flask.

– Is there anything else you remember about his appearance? Or anything else at all?
   – No…
   – Nothing that you specially reacted to?
   – No… Well, he smelled of alcohol.
   – Was he drunk?
   – Yes, I think so.
   – Was he visibly affected, so he had difficulty speaking

and walking, or did you react mostly to the smell?

– It was mostly the smell. And he had a bottle in his inner pocket.

– What kind of bottle?

– A small, flat one. A pocket flask or whatever it's called.

– And that one he kept in the inner pocket of his jacket?

– Yes.

– How did you know he had it there, then? Did he take it out?

– No, I felt it when he pressed himself against me.

I am trying to forget him, but it's impossible. It feels like I am tied to him with an invisible rope. No matter how much I twist and turn, I can't get loose. I don't know how to get rid of him.

When I am out among people my eyes are drawn to all light haired and short-cropped guys without me thinking of it. Even though my brain is occupied with other things, my eyes are searching. Why is that? I don't want to find him.

What would I do if I saw him? Go and call the police? But he would have disappeared before the police got there. And I couldn't walk up to him and force him with me or ask another person to hold him while I went away and called.

If I were sure he didn't recognize me, I could perhaps start talking with him and try to find out his name, but I don't know how much about me he remembers.

Or should I follow him and hope he was on his way home?

No, I don't want to find him.

Sometimes when I think it's him I see in the crowd, there is a twinge in my stomach and I get afraid he will catch sight of me, but otherwise I am not afraid. I wasn't really afraid when it happened either, though he was so threatening. I felt sorry for him. To be able to do as he did, you must be very lonely and unhappy, I think. I have thought that it wasn't sex he was after but love. His mother may have rejected him when he was little and needed her, so that he must try to force others to love him now. I don't mean that I think he had the right to do what he did, but I can't hate him for it.

But I should. I don't want to feel sorry for him and be forbearing and forgiving, but I don't know what to do about it. If I have buried what I actually feel, I don't know how to bring it out. You can't compel yourself to feel. It's maybe a defence mechanism that makes me unable to do it. I don't know. I am so stupid.

The stupidest thing is that I think what happened was *interesting*. I am ashamed to think so and I don't understand why I do it, but that's how it feels. I think it was an interesting experience. And I feel proud: This much I can handle without being cracked! And remarkable: You don't know what I have been through! And flattered: Of all who were out that evening he chose just me!

I can't be quite right in the head to think and feel like that! It's not normal. Instead of flattered and proud I should be sorry. But I am not. I can't.

I got a lift from Göran home from work. I get that rather often since he lives in the same direction as me. He has an apartment on Johannesbäcksgatan, and Bernt and I live on Gröna gatan. Bernt doesn't know that I mostly go with Göran, because he always comes home later than me, and I don't have a habit of talking about my workmates with him.

Göran and I don't talk very much either. He is older than me and may think we don't have much in common. We mostly listen to music in the car.

This time he first sat quite as usual, but then he looked a little extra at me and said:

"How are you?"

"I'm fine", I said.

"You haven't had any more books fall on you then?"

I felt stupid and didn't know what to answer, because I know he didn't believe that a book had fallen from a shelf.

And suddenly I got the idea that I should tell him about it. I got nervous just thinking it. My heart started beating faster, and I became completely shaky. Because I didn't know at all how he would take it. Good God, how do you say it? I thought. It can't be said! There he sat, thinking that Bernt had beaten me, and so I would say that I have been attacked and almost raped. But I couldn't do it, so it came to nothing.

I am almost sure that he believes I lied to protect Bernt, and I don't want him to suspect that about me, but I have myself to blame because I didn't get the truth out. I know there are more women than you believe who are raped, and that you don't have to be ashamed if it happens to you, but it still feels that way.

And you never know how people will react. Not that I believe that Göran would judge me and think it was my own fault, but he would perhaps feel sorry for me, and I couldn't bear that.

I can't stop thinking about it. Sometimes I see it like in a movie, where the camera comes closer and closer to what is happening. At the same time as I am in the film, I stand outside and watch. When Göran and I passed Lucullus, I thought about when I sat in there before the police came. I saw it in front of me. The empty police car on the street, the entrance to the restaurant, the crowd of people in the cloakroom… When we were on our way out to the police car, and people saw me coming there together with the police officers, I thought everyone could think that I had committed a crime or that I was a drug addict or an alcoholic, and then I was ashamed.

It cut like a knife in me when the memory images appeared, and a sound I couldn't stop came out of my mouth. Göran looked at me and asked what it was and was almost about to stop the car. It felt like I was going to choke, and I tried to cough a couple of times to get rid of it, but it didn't help.

Sometimes I can get the idea that I am in love with Göran, and that he is in love with me. I know it's because he is kind and seems a little interested in me, but that doesn't have to mean anything. It feels like he cares about me. And maybe he does, but not in the way I think. I get that. And I almost can't bear it. But I want to have it, so at the same time I enjoy it. I am so silly.

I am thinking about what happened almost all the time. I can't stop the memory images from appearing.

When everything was settled at the police station, I thought I would have to take a taxi home, but I got to go with a policeman in his private car. He gave me a lift when he was going home himself. By then it was after three o'clock in the morning. It was him I had been interrogated by last, so he knew everything, but he said nothing more about it but tried to talk about other things to divert my mind. I answered only briefly, because I couldn't be polite and sit and converse as if nothing had happened.

– There aren't so many out this time of day.
   – No.
   – Most of them are at home sleeping.
   – Yes.
   – But for some others it's active work time.
   – Yes.

I had no long trousers and no shoes on, and my feet

felt like pieces of ice. He had turned on the heat, but I froze anyway and felt strange. It was unpleasant to sit there and not know what he was thinking. I was alone with him in the car, and he had the power to do what he wanted. I don't know why I was thinking like that, because I didn't believe he was dangerous. After all, he was a policeman, and he knew what had happened. But once I read about a doctor who raped a girl whom he was to examine after a rape. Though that can't be true, because a doctor, who is there to help others and who everyone trusts, can't act that way. Not a policeman either.

When we arrived at home, he stopped the car by the sidewalk and waited for me to climb out.

— Do you live alone, or do you have someone with you now when you get home?
— My guy is home.
— That's good. Hope you can sleep now.
— Yes. Bye-bye and thanks for the lift.

I didn't want to go in to Bernt, but I had nowhere else to go, and when I came in, he was awake and asked where I had been. I didn't want to talk about it, because he felt so angry.

I still don't want to. The worst thing is that I don't feel like having sex with him either. I do it anyway, because I think I must, but I don't feel anything. I haven't wanted to admit it before, but when he got that upset and said he would go out and look for the guy in town, I felt that it could just as well have been him who had struggled with me. I don't know why, because he has never been violent or tried to force himself on me. It felt like he said he would go out and find the one who had molested me just because he thought that was how he *should* react, and not because he felt that way.

Göran gave me a lift home, and when I smelled the mixture of his after shave and the smoke from my cigarette in the car, I was reminded of how it was when I sat in the cloakroom at Lucullus and waited for the police to come. There was a murmur of voices and sounds around us, but I heard what the guy who had helped me there talked about with a guy who worked there, because both were standing right next to me.

– Can she remain sitting here? She isn't in the way?

  – No, no problem. Does she feel bad?

  – Yes, there is someone who has jumped on her and tried to rape her.

  – Rape?

  – Yes.

  – Oh, shit. Has someone called the cops then?

  – Yes, they are on their way.

  – Was it you who found her?

  – Yes, a little while ago. She came stumbling out of a gateway, completely apathetic.

  – Nearby?

– Yes, a bit up the street here.
– Had she been thrown out of a car?
– No, it happened in a back yard.

I didn't want to think about it, and perhaps I made a movement that made Göran notice that I felt uncomfortable, because he looked at me and asked what it was. It sounded as if he didn't mean only just then, but on the whole, and I don't know why, but when I heard his tone, I was almost ready to cry and had to turn away so that he wouldn't see that I was sad. I couldn't answer but just sat there staring out the window struggling to hold back my tears. Then he stopped the car and asked once more what it was.

But I couldn't tell him. I don't know him very well, and we have never talked about any personal things before. The only thing I know about him is that his sister died in a car accident some years ago. It isn't he himself who has told me, but Viola, who did it when I was new at the office. I haven't thought so much about it, and I have never talked with him about it, but now that this has happened, I understand how terrible he must have had it. It wasn't he who caused the accident, but he was the one driving when it occurred. He himself was only slightly injured, but his sister died, and what has happened to me is almost nothing compared with that.

I didn't dare tell him and said we would move

on. But when he started the car and drove away, I became disappointed, because deep down I had hoped he would persist.

In the evening when I had gone to bed, I thought about how it would have felt if he had hugged and comforted me, and then I became sad again and felt that I want him to do that.

As soon as Bernt touches me it's just sex. He can't put his arms around me without pressing his lower body against me at the same time. And I have never reacted to it because I have never experienced anything else. I have never known how it can be because papa never hugged and kissed me. When I got older and started to go out and meet guys, I thought it should be that way. I didn't realize that a guy can be tender and caring without involving sex in it. That he can be so that you feel that you don't have to be on your guard against him as soon as he approaches.

Bernt has told his parents about it. But he couldn't tell any details, because he hasn't been told any details. He doesn't know how far from, or how close, it was. He doesn't know what I thought and felt. He doesn't know how it happened. He doesn't *know*, and I am not going to tell him either.

I thought that Rut sat and watched me furtively, and when she talked with me, she had a comforting and reassuring tone that she doesn't use otherwise. And Olle avoided looking at me, I thought, and talking to me also, as if he were afraid I would come out with everything if I only got the opportunity. I tried to act as usual so that no one would feel compelled to ask how I felt or ask me to tell. I knew that no one would be able to handle it.

I think it was unnecessary of Bernt to tell them. I asked him later why he had done it and what he had said.

"What do you mean?" he said. "I said that a bastard came and jumped on you in town. Because that's how it was, wasn't it?"

I become sad when he talks like that, as if he suspects me of lying to him. I don't get why he does. Why must he be so hostile? It feels like he thinks I have insulted him, and that he can't forgive me. But it wasn't my fault that it happened. Anyway, I didn't agree to it, as he seems to believe.

Was I violated, molested, attacked, or assaulted? I don't know what to call it. The only thing I know is that I should have defended myself more.

I have been thinking about what I could have done to get away. I struggled against him and tried to come loose the entire time, except in the beginning when I didn't understand what he was going to do, but he was stronger than me, and he got angry and just grabbed me harder.

I know there are certain things you can do to perhaps get away, such as run up a knee between his legs or squeeze his testicles with your hands. But what if you squeezed them too loosely, so it didn't work and he got even angrier? And I have a resistance to using violence. If I get very angry I can perhaps do it but not otherwise.

And I didn't feel angry with him. I don't know why. In the beginning, I didn't understand what he was after, and later on I didn't think he would try to force me. I thought the whole time that I could get away. Why was I so stupid? I took for granted that it would be possible to talk with him. Before he thumped my head against the wall I said:

"Why are you doing this? It won't work anyway. If I scream people will come here and you will be caught. They will call the police. So, it's just as well if you release me and let me go."

I tried to give him a chance to stop before it was too late and make him understand that I wasn't angry and wouldn't report him if he didn't do more.

I didn't tell the police that I did that way.

But he didn't care what I said. It was probably not until then I began to understand that I might not be able to get off. So, in a way it was my own fault that it got as far as it did. Before I had understood that he was serious I didn't struggle as much as I could, and then it was too late.

– Didn't you try to attract attention by shouting for help when he grabbed you?
   – No.
   – Why not?
   – Because I didn't think it would be as it became later.
   – You didn't realize the seriousness of the situation?
   – No.

First, I didn't even scream. And I have read that a scream can just as well frighten a rapist, so it can make him try to silence his victim by resorting to even more serious violence.

And he got angry and hit me when I screamed.

But as long as we were out on the street I could have tried to get away, because there he had probably not dared to knock me down. But you don't start screaming and calling for help just because a person seizes you by the arm. And I don't know if there were people there either, who would have heard it and cared about it.

– Can you recall if any other people were on the street at this time?
   – No, I don't know.
   – You saw no one passing by or staying nearby?
   – No.

I know I should have offered more resistance so that he wouldn't have got me into that yard. When he seized me by the arm, I should have torn myself loose and walked away. But I didn't understand what he wanted.

– Didn't you understand then that it was intercourse he was after?
   – No, I didn't think so.
   – How was he in his conduct towards you, then?
   – I don't know… I suppose he got angry because I didn't want to stay and talk.
   – You got the impression that he was angry?
   – Yes, or annoyed.
   – And what was it that gave you that impression?
   – That he sounded angry in his voice and grabbed my

arm when I started walking.

– But he didn't behave so threateningly that you considered it justified to call for help?

– No.

Mamma called and wanted us to come over for dinner. I didn't feel like it, but Bernt thought we should go, because we haven't been there for a long time.

I didn't want to because it felt like I wouldn't be able to stand her talking. Why does she talk so much all the time? About things she has bought and read and heard and seen on TV. She goes on and on without interruption and believes that everyone should be interested and want to listen.

But I don't want to. If what she said were important, or if she could listen herself sometimes, it would perhaps feel different, but she never does. I know I am as self-absorbed as she just now and only dwell on things, but I am not forcing anyone else to listen to it, anyway. And in normal circumstances I mostly listen to others. I have always done that. But now I feel like I am getting tired of letting people take advantage of me. Because they who like talking talk with just everyone.

I can't stand listening to mamma forever. Sometimes when I call her I do it a quarter of an hour before a TV program that I have intended to see, so that it won't be so long lasting if she should start expatiating.

First, I ask her how she is, because I think you should do that when you call someone, even if she never asks me about it. Well, she perhaps asks sometimes, but it isn't because she wants to know how I am that she gets in touch. And mostly she starts right away by talking about herself. She answers questions that I haven't asked, and that feels so weird. "Well, I'm just fine. No, otherwise nothing special has happened." She can just as well sit and talk to a wall if she doesn't even need me to ask questions before she answers.

Why is she so self-absorbed? I thought about it before Bernt and I went to her and decided that I wouldn't listen to more than I wanted to, if possible. The only way is almost to go out or lock yourself in the bathroom, because if you only go into another room, she might follow you.

But it didn't turn out the way I had expected. I was sad and felt negative, and she noticed it, and therefore she turned to Bernt almost the whole time instead. She just ignored me and treated me as if I didn't exist.

I could never tell mamma about the attempted rape. She would just think I had myself to blame and not listen. She perhaps doesn't believe that you attract rapists by being sexy and defiantly dressed, or by behaving in a certain way towards men you meet, but she thinks you should be careful and avoid lonely places if you have to go out when it's dark and rather not be out alone. So, I know she would think it was my own fault.

I don't think the police will find the one who attacked me. And I don't care about it either. Because if he is caught, there will be a trial, and then I must attend it and I don't know if I want to do that.

I wouldn't have reported it if that guy hadn't come and helped me. He was the one who called the police, and then I was obliged to complete it. But I would never have reported it myself. I just wanted to go home and forget all of it. Then no one would have needed to know.

– Hello there. What's happened to you, then?

– …

– Do you feel unwell? Do you need help?

– No, I…

– What's happened?

– …

– Has someone fought with you?

– Yes, but that's nothing to worry about.

– Well, I think it is.

– …

– Do you live nearby?

– No.

– How did you end up here, then?

– I have been to the cinema.

– And then someone came and started fighting with you?

He wondered what had happened, but I just thought of my bag with the money and the bus card and the keys and asked if he could come with me into the yard and pick them up.

And he did. My clothes were scattered on the ground, and the gravel where we had been standing was torn so it appeared that some people had fought there, and when he caught sight of it I was embarrassed and felt stupid.

I went ahead and picked up the bag. When I was about to take the coat as well, he said it was probably best to leave the rest until the police had been there. I hadn't thought of the police, but then I understood that I couldn't just take the clothes and go home.

He helped me out on the street and into Lucullus, and there he called. I had to sit on a chair in the cloakroom and wait until the police arrived. It was full of people there, but no one cared about me, except for a waitress who came over and tried to talk to me.

– How do you feel?

– I'm okay.

– Is there anything I can do?
– No.
– Would you like anything?
– No, it's okay.
– Sure?
– Yes.
– Yes, I won't bother you. Soon the police will be here,
and so you can talk to them instead.

I just wanted to disappear. I was ashamed of what I looked like and because I didn't have any long trousers on. The ankle socks looked so silly with the cardigan. It would have been better if I had been barefoot, because then it wouldn't have been so noticeable that the trousers were missing. But I didn't dare take off my socks.

And the police came.

– Hello. What's happened here, then?
– ...
– Someone has jumped on her and tried to rape her.
– Is this true? Can you confirm that it is as it's said here now?
– ...
– Can you tell me what happened?
– ...
– She's probably in shock.
– Mm. But she has stated that she has been subjected to an attempted rape?
– Yes, she said something like that. And considering

how little clothes she has on, it's probably true.

– Mm. So, it was you who found her and brought her here?

– Yes.

– What time was it?

– About half past eleven.

– And where was she when you first caught sight of her?

– A bit up the street here. She was completely apathetic.

– Mm. And you saw no one else nearby?

– No, no one I thought of.

– No, okay. … Can you tell us now what happened?

– …

– She's probably in shock.

– Mm. … What's your name? Can you tell me your name?

– …

– Has someone been nasty to you?

– Yes.

– Who?

– I don't know.

– It was no one you know, then? No one you are familiar with since before or have seen before?

– No.

– And you haven't suffered serious bodily injury, so you need to go to the hospital?

– No.

– Yes, now you will soon come with us, here.

It was probably not until then I understood how serious everyone thought it was and that I had to help.

When we were about to leave and came out on the street, we had to walk past people who had gathered there. One of the policemen opened the door to the back seat of the police car and let me sit there before he climbed in beside me, and the other one sat behind the wheel and started talking on the radio. I thought I could relax then, and tried to lie down on the seat, but I wasn't permitted, because first I had to give a description of the perpetrator so that a police message could be sent out.

It felt so strange to sit there, in a police car on the way to the police station in the middle of the night. I had nothing to do with the hard nightlife on the streets and should have been at home sleeping instead.

The police officers tried to make me relax by talking about other things – the one sitting next to me asked a little about the movie I had been to – and I answered as best as I could, but I didn't want to sit and pretend like everything was as usual when it wasn't. I wasn't aware of it right then, but when I think about it now, I get sad. I wanted to know what I felt. Why wasn't I allowed to do that? Why was I hindered? The policemen should have helped me to feel instead of trying to distract me.

I can't stand mamma's phone calls. She doesn't call because she is interested in *me*, and if she has nothing new to say, she just repeats the same old trifles as the time before. I don't understand what she wants. It creeps inside me, and I must compel myself to listen.

She is just talking. Why can't she take time to listen a little also? It feels like she doesn't care about me when she never asks anything about me. She may expect me to tell myself, as *she* does, but I have no confidence in her and know she wouldn't be interested, so I don't even try.

She is my mother, but sometimes it feels like I detest her because she always takes up so much space with her talk. She only thinks of herself and leaves no room for others. Last time I went to her I had a newly baked sponge cake with me, but she didn't even thank me when I gave it to her. And when we had coffee, she said nothing about how it tasted either. I don't mean that it's too much that I take a cake with me when I come, but couldn't she at least show that she notices it?

The only right thing to do would be to stop see-
ing her. Why should I be nice to her when she isn't
nice to me? I don't know why I don't object. I feel
like I am just being used when I compel myself to
listen to her.

I didn't get to know what I felt. It was shut in, and now it can't be brought out. I just feel tense and irritable. I try not to show it to Bernt, but I know he notices it all the same.

It only took a few minutes to drive to the police station. When we got there, one of the policemen asked if I wanted to call home and tell where I was. I hadn't thought of Bernt, but then I thought that he was probably asleep, and that it wouldn't be long before I could go home and that it was unnecessary to wake him. And I was afraid he would feel compelled to come there if he found out where I was, and I didn't want that.

I got to sit in a chair in front of a desk, and on the other side the police officer from the back seat sat down and began to write a report. He took out a form that he started to fill in.

– We start with your name. What's your name?
  – Susanne Holmkvist.
  – Do you have several first names?
  – Yes, Eva also.

– Eva Susanne? In that order?
– Yes.
– And what do you work with?
– I work in an office.
– In an office… And what's your social security number?

It felt like I was going to choke. My heart pounded so hard that my ears were buzzing. It was strenuous to stay up and not get to relax and feel. But there was no time for that. Or if no one believed I needed it because I seemed so composed. It felt like everyone thought that the only important thing was that I as soon as possible told them what had happened. And I wanted it too, but it would have felt better if I could have rested a little first.

I asked if smoking was allowed, and then I got an ashtray. When I lit the cigarette, I saw that I had blood on my fingers. I didn't know where it came from, and it felt disgusting to have it on me. But I wasn't allowed to wash it off. I saw a washbasin in a corner and got up to go there, but the policeman stopped me.

– Just a minute! Where are you going?
– I'm going to wash my hands.
– Unfortunately, I must ask you to wait with that until after the medical examination. There may be traces that can be used as evidence against a possible…
– Yes, I didn't think of that.

– It's okay. And after the examination you are to look at some photos while you still have his appearance fresh in your memory.

– Yes.

– Shall we continue then?

After that I had to tell what had happened. But it got so messy, because when I had said one thing, and he had written it down, I came up with something else that had happened before that.

– He pushed me up against a wall and tried to pull up my sweater. No, first he unbuttoned my coat. But there was a lamp there, so he pushed me in where it was darker and pressed me up against another wall. That's when he pulled up my sweater and took out... First, he pressed me against the wall with his body and then...

And I couldn't help thinking about how it felt for him to hear me tell about it. He may also have found it unpleasant. He was rather young and seemed embarrassed and almost apologetic sometimes, as if he were ashamed of what he was doing. I felt sorry for him, but there was nothing I could do about it since it was his job to question me.

– And what happened next?

– He tore off my briefs.

– Describe how he did it.

– He put both hands inside the elastic at the top and

pulled so the cloth was torn to pieces and fell off.

– And what did he do after that?

– He pulled the zipper down on his fly.

– Yes, and then?

– … he took out…

– His male organ?

– Yes.

– What did you do then?

– I screamed.

– Did you call for help or was it just a cry without words?

– Just a cry.

– And how did he react to that?

– He got angry and hit me.

– Where? Where did the blow hit?

– In my face.

I felt dirty in my face and thought I smelled bad. I wanted to go and wash myself, but I knew it wasn't permitted and tried not to think about it.

After a while, a doctor came and examined me. I felt guilty because he had been awakened and called there in the middle of the night just because of me. He looked so tired, and his hair was untidy, as if he hadn't given himself time to comb before he left.

I had only got some bruises and abrasions and wasn't seriously injured, but you are examined all the same, so that a medical report can be written. It's needed as proof. I had to stand under a strong lamp while he did the examination.

– Do you have pain somewhere?
– I don't know.
– I understand that you feel bruised, but besides that?
– No, just that it is a little sore here in the back of my head.
– Yes, you have a contusion here.
– And it hurts when I swallow.
– Would you please open your mouth? Thanks, that's good. Have you had anything inserted into your mouth?
– No.
– And now I must ask you to take off your clothes.

A woman police was with us the whole time. Sometimes a gynaecological examination is also done, but it's only needed if it is a completed rape. If that's the case, they look for injuries in the vagina and take samples to find remnants of semen. Sometimes the injuries are photographed, but no one photographed me. The doctor described what he saw in words instead and recorded it on a tape.

– The conjunctiva of the eyes pale, the pupils medium dilated and equally large … no bleeding … in the oral cavity and nasal cavities there is no foreign content … on the back of the head there is a minor contusion caused by external, blunt violence … on the left cheek just below the eye a walnut-sized bluish swelling … on the neck slight redness … over both shoulders down towards the

collarbones linear, approximately 6 centimetre long, 1 centimetre wide, subcutaneous bleeding … on the left breast an approximately 2 x 2 cm subcutaneous bleeding … on the upper extremities an area with patchy epidermal scrapes and subcutaneous bleeding … on the inside of both upper arms continuous hematomas, approximately 5 x 6 cm large … on the right hand some blood on the middle finger and back of the hand … on the back of the body over the hips with spread down over the buttocks a large area with epidermal abrasions and bruises … on both the lower extremities various scratches, abrasions and bruises … on the outside of the right thigh an approximately 6 x 8 cm large hematoma … on the inside of both thighs stains of dried blood as well as a number of point-shaped bruises about 1.5 cm in diameter…

Otherwise, I don't know what he did. I don't know if he found any traces or if he took any samples. I don't know what kind of room we were in, and I don't know how long we were in there. The only thing I remember is that I was standing under a strong lamp while he examined me.

When the examination was over and I had dressed again, I was allowed to go to the toilet. For security reasons I wasn't permitted to lock the door behind me.

It burned when I peed. I didn't want to look at myself in the mirror. I washed my hands and face. I felt overwrought and completely shaky, but I wanted to stay at the police station as long as possible, because later I would be alone and not able to talk about it anymore. With the police I could talk, and I got help to go through it in the smallest detail, but later there wouldn't be anyone I could tell. I didn't think about it, but I had a feeling of how it was going to be, and that's why I didn't want to go home.

When I got back to the first room, I was to sit at a table and look at photos of criminals. A policeman brought me thick albums to go through. I thought I would recognize him if I saw him again, but he wasn't there.

It was the first time I was inside a police station. People came and went all the time. Policemen and arrested persons, crime victims and drunks. I tried to concentrate on the photos, but what was happening around distracted me, and it felt like everyone was looking at me. I thought that the police officers who came in probably knew what had happened out in town and understood that it was me who had come up against the guy they were looking for in the radio patrol cars, and that they were aware that I was sitting there without any briefs on under my long cardigan. I had nothing on my legs either, and no shoes, and I was dirty and ugly. When I think about it now I am ashamed, although I know I couldn't help it.

Finally, I had to tell everything again to another, plain-clothes man who was a detective inspector and much older than the first one. He took me away from the desk where I had been sitting with the albums and into another room. When he noticed that I looked at the closed door he said:

"If you prefer us to leave the door open, we can do that, but I thought it would feel better for you if we could talk undisturbed."

"Yes, it's okay this way," I said.

But it wasn't, because I was so aware that he was a man, and that I was alone with him in there.

– I know you've already told it once, but it's important, you know, that we get a very clear picture of what happened.

– Yes.

– You come walking on Vaksalagatan in the direction towards Vaksala torg when you pass by a male who has taken his stand at the street corner of Storgatan outside the electrical shop?

– Yes.

– Can you please give an account of the continued course of events as accurately as possible.

– Yes, and when I had walked a bit, I heard steps behind me and a voice that said: "Wait a minute!"

– And what do you do then?

– I turn around.

– Do you stop, or do you keep walking?

– I keep walking. But he caught up with me and asked if I knew what time it was.

– And then you stopped?

– Yes, and looked at my watch. But as soon as I had said the time, I started walking again.

– And what time was it? Do you remember that?

– Yes, it was around half past ten.

– Around 22.30.

– Yes.

– And what happens after that?

– He started walking beside me.

– And?

– I don't know… I increased the pace, I think.

– You started walking faster.

– Yes, and then he said: "You don't have to be in such a hurry, do you? Stop and chat for a while." But I didn't want to do that, and he got angry and seized me by the arm.

– In what way did you show that you weren't interested?

– I said it. "We have nothing to talk about", I said.

– And then he grabbed your arm?

– Yes, and said once more that he wanted it.

– Wanted to chat with you?

I didn't quite understand why the review had to be so detailed, but I answered as best as I could to everything he asked.

– He holds you fast with one hand and unbuttons your coat with the other?

– Yes. And then he pushed me against the wall with his body.

– Does he say anything in connection with him doing this?

– No.

– In what state of mind does he seem to be, then?

– I don't know…

– Would you say that he took up a threatening attitude?

– No, not right then. He seemed most… determined.

– Determined.

– Yes.

– And then what happened?

– Then he pulled up my sweater.

– Describe how he did it.

– He pulled it up through the neckline of my cardigan. It goes down like this over the whole…

– Yes, I understand. And then?

– He took a breast out of the bra and bent down and kissed it.

I can no longer hide that I don't enjoy it when Bernt has sex with me. I don't want to let him do it anymore. The only difference from a rape is that I don't resist. He doesn't have to force himself on me. But if I objected maybe he would? He is perhaps after the same thing as that guy was, though it isn't noticeable because I am not protesting? What he wants, may have nothing to do with me, and that's perhaps why I can't respond.

If I had agreed to have sex with that guy instead of fighting back, it might have felt about the same as it does when I sleep with Bernt. So why did I offer resistance? If I hadn't done that I would have avoided being beaten, and letting him have sex with me might not have been so bad. I should perhaps have done as Egon once said: "If a broad is being raped, she can just as well lie down and enjoy it while it's going on."

If I said no to Bernt he would probably not hit me, but it would surely end between us. And how would I explain it? I can't say that he is like a rapist and that's why I don't want to sleep with him. I can't prove that it's him there is something wrong with. The most likely is that I am frigid. That's what *he* would say anyway, if I told him that I don't feel very much when we have sex.

I have done it now. I have said no to Bernt. When he wanted to lay me, I said that I didn't want to. Before, sometimes, when I have wanted to avoid it, I have alleged fatigue and headaches as an excuse, but now I said straight out that I didn't feel like it. I thought I could take advantage of the situation and blame it on the attempted rape, even though I know that it actually has nothing to do with it. Not in that way anyway. When he asked me why I said:

"I suppose I'm frigid."

I couldn't say that I suspect it's due to him, because it can't be just his fault, and I still don't know what it is with me that causes it. But I know he thinks that having sex with me is the only thing that matters and not how it feels. The only thing he cares about is getting his sexual needs satisfied, and he thinks I owe him help with that.

When I think of all who don't see and respect me, it feels like I don't want to be a part of that anymore. I don't want to let it happen again. It's you yourself who must object and show that you don't accept it.

There is both physical and mental rape, but the

mental one is seldom thought of, though it's probably more common than the physical one. And it isn't punishable either. Besides, they are connected. If you have a bad self-esteem you don't think you are worth that much and don't defend yourself enough physically either, if you are attacked. Because it is yourself and not just your body you try to defend.

You should not differentiate between body and soul, but to protect yourself you may do so. Either you disconnect your soul and concentrate on what you feel in your body, or you do the opposite. And you do it to avoid realizing that you don't get everything you need. If you experienced the whole, you might have to admit that you are completely alone, and you don't want to do that.

As soon as I am alone, I think about it. I go through it in my mind and try to get it in order. It feels like I haven't comprehended it yet and need to repeat it until it becomes clearer.

I had been to the cinema, at the last show, and when I was on my way to the bus afterwards, I met him. I was walking on Vaksalagatan, down under the railroad viaduct and up the hill, and at the corner of Storgatan I saw a guy standing and smoking. It felt a little unpleasant to have to pass him, because guys often come out with a comment when you walk by, but I didn't want to be a coward, so I moved on.

And he didn't say anything. But when I had passed him, he came after me and grabbed my arm and asked what time it was. Yes, and I stopped and said it and started walking again. Then he followed me.

– On which side of you did he walk in relation to the street?

– On the left side closest to the curb.

– To your left. Does he say anything in connection with him starting to walk next to you, or is he quiet?

– He was quiet.

– And what did you think? What conclusions did you draw from his behaviour?

At first, I thought he did it because he was going in the same direction as me, but then I realized that he wanted company. And I was so stupid, because then I began to think about how he looked and how he seemed to be, about the same as you do when you are out dancing and being asked. You kind of feel if the guy makes a positive or a negative impression. While judging him, I began to walk faster and tried to look uninterested. Then he said:

"You don't have to be in such a hurry, do you? Stop and chat for a while."

"We have nothing to talk about," I said, and maybe I sounded snooty, because he grabbed my arm and held it so I had to stop again.

"I want to chat with you!" he said and shoved me against the wall.

– Shoved?

– Yes, or pushed. I struggled against him and tried to free myself, but he just…

– You offered resistance?

– Yes, but he didn't let go.

He pushed me into a gateway and blocked my way

so I couldn't get out on the street again. I held on to the closed half of an iron gate that was there, because I didn't want to go in there with him. He tried to tear lose my hands, and when that didn't work, he put one hand in his jacket pocket and pushed out the cloth towards me and said:

"I have a pistol!"

But I didn't believe him, because why would he walk around with a gun on him? I thought he held out the jacket with a finger.

– He points an object, which he keeps hidden under his jacket, at you and tries to claim he has a firearm?

– Yes.

– And how did you react to that?

– I got afraid.

– But you never saw the weapon?

– No.

I said to the police that I was afraid, but I wasn't.

"We're going in here!" he said and knocked me, so I lost my grip on the gate.

"Why?" I said.

"Because I say so!"

Then he pushed me into the yard and pressed me up against a wall and unbuttoned my coat and pulled up my sweater. I felt completely bewildered and didn't understand what was happening. I reacted so slowly. But at last, when he had got my long trousers down, I tried to object.

– He pulled down your long trousers?

– No, not pulled. He opened the button at the waist and pulled down the zipper, and for that reason they went down by themselves.

– The trousers went down?

–Yes, to my feet. At first, I let them lie there, but then I stepped out of them so that I could run away if I would get the opportunity.

– I see. And then?

– I don't know. I don't remember.

– Take it easy. We are in no hurry. So, you had stepped out of your trousers?

– Yes, and my shoes.

– You had taken off your shoes as well?

– Yes, because otherwise I wouldn't have been able to get rid of my long trousers.

– No. And then what happened?

– Then he tried to pull down my briefs. When he did that I screamed, and he got angry and hit me in the face. Then he seized me by the throat.

– Can you describe how he held his hands?

– Yes, with one hand on each side of my neck.

– With his thumbs on the front over your throat?

– Yes.

– Was it a hard grip, or…?

– No, it was just a hold.

– He didn't squeeze so you had difficulty breathing?

– No.

– He did not. Does he say anything in connection with

him applying this hold on you?

   – Yes. "If you shout again, I'll kill you!" he said.

He thumped my head against the wall. At that moment I realized that he was serious. I hadn't really understood it before, but then I realized that he might not let me go until he had had his will. I started talking to him and said everything I could think of that I thought could make him change his mind.

   But he didn't listen. He tried to pry my legs apart and get my briefs down, and he was so strong, and it was so exhausting to fight, so at last I wouldn't be able to do it any longer, I knew. That's probably when I suggested I could masturbate him.

– You suggested you would try to give him an ejaculation with the help of your hand?

   – Yes, because I thought that if he… if he got an ejaculation, he would perhaps be satisfied with it and let me be.

   – And how did he respond to your suggestion?

   – "Yes, do it then, damn it!" he said.

   – And what happened?

   – I tried, but he had almost no erection, and I became so tired in my arm.

I don't know how long I carried on with it. Finally, I couldn't take it anymore and let go. Because I noticed that it wouldn't succeed. But he had been

aroused by it, although it wasn't visible, and tore
off my briefs. Then he tried to get it in.

– Can you describe a little more closely how he acted?
–Yes, first he stuck in his fingers. I held my legs to-
gether, but he put a hand there and stuck in…
– He stuck his fingers into the vagina?
– Yes.
– Were there two or more fingers?
– Two, I think. I tore and pulled at his hand to remove
it, but it didn't work, and he placed himself closer and
tried to put in… tried to exchange his fingers for…
– His penis?
– Yes, and I… "You may not!" I said.
– "Yes, it must go in!" he said.
– Did he say exactly that?
– Yes.
– Because it's important, you know, considering his
intent.
– That's what he said.
– Okay.

PART THREE

Now the police have found a guy who could be the one who assaulted me. A policeman called and informed me about it and asked me to come to the police station to participate in a witness confrontation. I am going there today after work. If it's him, I am almost certain I will recognize him, because I saw him clearly. But what happens if he doesn't confess? Will he be released then, or is it enough that I say it's him?

If there will be a trial, I must attend it. I don't want that. I may not even get any questions but have to tell everything myself, and I can't do that. If there are several people listening at the same time, I can't talk.

I hope it's not him. But if it is, he will see me at the trial. He was under the influence of alcohol when it happened and may not remember how I looked, and when he sees me again, he might think: How the hell could I get at that ugly chick?

Why do I think like that when I don't mean it? I don't care what he thinks of me. It's rather me who should think that *he* is ugly and disgusting. It's *he* who should be afraid of what *I* would think of *him* and not the other way around!

But I can't feel it. And everyone else may also think: Why didn't he choose a prettier girl while he was at it? I know I am not ugly, and I know I don't care what others think of my appearance, so why do I think like that? What's wrong with me? Why am I so weird?

Two police officers followed me into a dark room where there was a large window on one wall. Through the window you could see into another room where seven guys were lined up under a strong lamp.

– You can walk up to the mirror and see if you recognize any of the persons in the adjoining room. Just take it easy and remember that none of those on the other side of the pane can see you.
– Yes, I…
– Take your time and look carefully at each one.
– Yes, but I already know it's number three.
– Number three. You recognize him?
– Yes, he's the one who did it.
– It was number three who attacked you?
– Yes.
– And you are absolutely sure about that?
– Yes.

I saw him immediately. He had different clothes

and some longer hair, and he was much heavier than I remembered him, but I recognized him as soon as I saw him. I don't know what I felt. Nothing, I think.

When I had pointed him out, I had to leave at once. It felt like it had happened too fast, but there wasn't anything more I needed to do. On the way out I asked how the police had managed to catch him, and then I was told that he had been arrested after a new attempted rape.

I hadn't thought of that there could be others. I thought I was the only one, and when I realized that I wasn't, I almost felt disappointed. I can't be quite right in the head! Why do I react so strangely? What's wrong with me?

I despise myself for being so weird. What he did, served me right. He could just as well have succeeded in raping me, because then I perhaps would have grasped it. First abused and then raped, so that I had been made to feel it properly.

Deep down, I perhaps *wanted* to have sex with him? Maybe I want it with anyone who seems interested in me? Maybe I am so flattered that I can't say no? Maybe I offered resistance just because I didn't dare to admit that?

And Bernt believes I agreed to it. When I came home from the police he said:

"Well, had they caught the right bull?"

As if a rapist would be a highly-sexed person I would like, and he would feel threatened by that.

But the guy in town didn't get hard even when I tried to excite him. Maybe I did it the wrong way. I didn't know how tight I should hold and how fast I should pull, because I had never done it before. And when it didn't work, I regretted that I had tried. But I thought he was aroused already before, and that it would go quickly and easily and that he would let me be afterwards.

Last Wednesday when I was sick and at home from work, the doorbell rang. I had a fever and was in bed, and I considered not opening, but I wondered who it was and got up and looked out through the peephole in the door. When I saw that it was Göran who was standing there, I was so surprised that I unlocked and opened before I had time to think about it. I had only my ugly bathrobe on, and my hair hung in fat wisps – I hadn't bothered to wash it, nor myself, so carefully while I was sick – and I had to let him see that.

He wanted to know how I felt, he said. He knew I was home alone, because when I called to work and reported myself sick, he was the one who answered, and I happened to mention that Bernt was on a course. But why did he come to my home?

He asked if he could come in, and then he followed me into the living room and sat down on the sofa. It was strange that he did it so naturally and effortlessly. I kind of couldn't believe that it was he who was sitting there, in our home, on the sofa in my and Bernt's living room.

After a while he got up and walked over to the bookcase and lifted a photo of Bernt.

"Is this your guy?" he said.

I could only nod, and he looked at me and said:

"Can you answer a question truthfully?"

He looked so serious that I almost got nervous.

"Yes, what?" I said.

"Is he hitting you?"

I couldn't help laughing.

"No, he isn't," I said. "Why do you ask?"

"I may not believe in storybooks."

At first, I didn't get it, but then I understood that he meant that he didn't believe I had got the bruise on my face from a book that had fallen from a shelf. He had seen that I had bruises in other places as well, he said.

Then I went and fetched the first newspaper clipping and let him read it. He was sitting on the sofa reading, and I was standing at the bookcase and was so nervous that I trembled. I heard my heartbeat in my ears, and I could hardly breathe.

When he looked up, I dared not look at him.

— Were you the one this happened to?

— Yes.

— But why haven't you told?

— I don't know.

— How bad was it?

— Not so bad.

— That's when you got the bruise on your face?

– Yes.
– Is he still at large?
– No, he is arrested now.

He asked some questions, but he didn't show what he felt, and I didn't know what he thought.

I still don't know. Maybe he felt sorry for me, because when he was about to leave, he hugged me. I wish I had dared to open then, and receive his consolation, but the only thing I could think was that I wasn't clean and maybe smelled bad and that he would feel it and think I was disgusting.

When he had left, I cried.

I still don't know why he came. He may have suspected that I was at home because Bernt had abused me so much that I couldn't show myself at work and came to see if it was true or not. Otherwise I don't understand.

At least now he knows the truth, and I don't regret telling him, because when I think about it, he is probably the only one of my acquaintances who I feel confidence in.

I have stopped smoking. I haven't smoked a single cigarette in eleven days, and I have never had such a long break before. It was when I was sick that I decided to try to quit.

The worst thing is that I have become so easily irritated and grumpy. I snap at Bernt and feel ready to cry for the smallest thing.

Last night when I was in the bathtub and saw my naked body in the water, it felt like I felt sorry for it and wanted to protect it. *Help me*, I thought. *Mom, why don't you come and help me?* I cried and called for mamma. At the same time as I called – or felt that I called, because I didn't do it loudly – I knew it wouldn't help. She wouldn't come. There was no point in trying.

First, I believed I was sorry because I had been assaulted, but actually it was because no one came and helped me – or that *mamma* has never helped me – that felt so unbearable. I don't really know how it could be like that. Maybe I was reminded of it when I needed help against that guy but didn't get it. I didn't call for help either, because I thought no one would care. And when I just screamed no one came, just as mamma never came when I was little.

No, I don't know. I thought of Göran also, and of what I think he would have done if he had been there. He would have helped me and comforted me and made sure that that guy had got his punishment. That's how it feels. But mamma wouldn't have helped me, and neither would Bernt.

I got a lift from Göran again. When we went on Vaksalagatan and came past the gate to number 25 I got the idea that I should go in there and look. I asked Göran if he wanted to come along. My heart started beating faster, and my legs became shaky, and when we came into the yard, I felt sick and almost thought I was going to faint.

And suddenly I remembered. Suddenly I knew that it didn't end as I had thought. It wasn't as I believed, that I got away, but he got hold of me again and threw me to the ground and raped me.

It was as if an abyss opened when the memory came back. I was completely stiff and covered my face with my hands. Göran came nearer and asked me what it was, but I couldn't answer.

"Come here," he said in a low voice, and when I heard his tone there was a thrill in my stomach. I went into his arms and let him hold me, and he tried to comfort and calm me, but I was completely stiff and couldn't receive it. When we sat in the car again, he asked if I wanted to talk about it, but I couldn't, and he drove me home.

And I went in to Bernt, who wondered why I was late and came out with that I perhaps had been out and become molested again, and I simply couldn't; I couldn't answer or care about what he said and just wanted him to disappear.

But he followed me into the bathroom, and into the kitchen, and into the bedroom, and he went on and on the whole time about what he thought I had been up to. I didn't listen, but I heard anyway, and everything was over, over, and he couldn't reach me, and therefore he did the only thing he believed would work, but that didn't work either, because I thought of Göran the whole time, and one or two times doesn't matter much, I thought.

No, he didn't rape me, but it wasn't far from it. He knew I didn't want to, but I didn't say no, and I didn't struggle against it, so I have to blame myself.

In the evening when I had gone to bed, I couldn't fall asleep. I thought about all that happened that night and couldn't relax. It was like watching a movie, because I saw it from the outside the whole time, as if it weren't me it was about.

I don't think I have really comprehended it yet. Not with feeling. Because it's one thing to remember what happened and another to feel what it was like. Images appear, and I remember voices and words, but I don't feel anything.

Now I must go to the police and tell them that it was a completed rape. If the guy has confessed, the police must wonder why I didn't say it like it was.

I must go there in any case, because if I don't tell the truth I will entangle myself when I am to tell at the trial what happened. I don't want him to be punished for less than he is guilty of either.

It might seem like I lied to protect him. But I didn't remember. I was completely convinced that I got away and ran out on the street and came across that guy who helped me into the restaurant later.

Now I have been to the police and told them how it really was. I have told the truth, the whole truth and nothing but the truth. When I was there previously, to fetch my clothes, a policeman gave me a visiting card with his name and telephone number, and that number I called before I went there. When I had told him what it was about, he said I could come the same day, and after lunch I went there. At work I said that I didn't feel well and needed to go home earlier. I haven't told Bernt what I have found out, so I thought it was best to do it during work time so that I wouldn't have to lie to him.

I got to meet the same policeman as last time. He came and picked me up at the entrance, and when we had entered his room he sat down at the desk and opened a folder which lay in front of him. He asked me to sit down and started a tape recorder and rattled off date and time and name and why I was there. After that I got to tell.

– In this situation, I must ask you questions that I don't like to ask. Some of them will be very personal and in-

discreet. It isn't my intention to embarrass or torment you, but I have to ask and get answers. Do you under-stand?

– Yes.

– Good. Take it from the beginning. Tell me what he did to you and how it happened.

– Should I take it from the very beginning or when he…

– When you tried to run away, he grabbed you again and knocked you to the ground?

– Yes, and then he sat down on me and hit me in the face.

– How did he sit down?

– With one leg on each side of me and his knees against the ground so I couldn't get up. First against the ground and then against my arms.

– He placed himself astride of you and pressed your arms down with his knees?

– Yes.

– And then he gave you a slap in the face?

– Yes.

– Did he strike with an open hand or a clenched fist?

– A clenched fist.

– And it was just one blow?

– Yes.

– Does he say anything in connection with dealing out this punch?

– Yes. "You sure as hell won't do that again!" he said.

I was afraid he would find it strange that I hadn't

remembered everything from the beginning, but he said that it isn't at all unusual for a person who has been involved in a traumatic event to suffer from memory loss. He or she forgets what has happened, completely or partially, as protection against emotional overload, and it's a completely normal defensive reaction, he said.

He was kind and understanding and made me feel that he and I were on the same side against that guy. It felt as if he was interested in me and wanted to help me. But it was probably just to get information he was interested in.

At least now I have done my duty and told everything that happened.

– Is there anything you want to add? Something you have wondered about or you think I've forgotten to ask?
– No...
– Okay. Then I'll thank you for coming here, and I'm turning off the tape recorder at 15.35.

When I got home, I felt strange. It felt like I hadn't told the truth although I had. It felt like I hadn't come to the most important thing. But I don't know what the most important thing is.

I become sad when I think about that policeman and his tone when he talked to me. I put compassion and consideration and respect and love, and I don't know what else, in his voice. But that couldn't have been there. I get that. There wasn't anything in it but professional interest. I had information, which it was his job to get out, and therefore he listened. It was only my information he was interested in and nothing else. He wasn't interested in *me,* because no one is.

Not even mamma and papa have been. If I had got what I needed when I was little, I might have avoided going here now and reacting so weirdly to everything. It feels as if that policeman cared more about me than papa did. A stranger, who didn't know me, cared more about me than he did. Because papa never listened and never had time. He was never there. I could never come to him and talk about what I was thinking of and filled with, because he never had time, and he wasn't interested, and didn't want to hear, and didn't want to know, and didn't want to *have* me, because he didn't love me.

Neither did Bernt. Was it perhaps because he was like papa that I fell for him? But now I don't want to be together with a person who doesn't care about me. Now I want to be with someone who listens and consoles and understands.

You must be able to defend yourself. To have a chance to get away if you are attacked, you must both feel that you are worth defending and know what to do. I have read about it in a book and tried to figure out what I should have done if I had known what were the right things to do.

Firstly, when I saw him standing there at the street corner smoking, and I thought it felt uncomfortable to have to pass him, I should just have crossed to the other side of the street. Because he had probably thought out in advance that he would try to get a girl into that back yard.

Secondly, when he stopped me and asked what time it was, I shouldn't have stopped but said that I didn't know and kept walking.

And when he started walking next to me, I should have gone to a place where there were a lot of people. I could, for instance, have turned back and gone into Lucullus.

And when he grabbed my arm, I should have pulled myself free or run my elbow into the side of him so that he had to let go of me.

But then he said he had a gun, and in that situation, I don't know what to do. But I didn't believe it, so I hadn't needed to worry about it.

I feel ashamed when I think of how weak I was. There are so many things I could have done. When he pushed me up against the wall, I could have kicked him or stamped on his foot or run my knee up between his legs and come free.

But what did I do? Oh yes, I was just standing there, waiting for him to quit on his own.

– You had no opportunity to get out of there?
– No.
– In what way did he hinder you?
– He held my arms and pressed me against the wall. I couldn't get loose and get past him.

The police officers who interrogated me must have thought I was stupid. It's true that he hit me when I tried to get loose, but I didn't do anything back. If you don't know what to do and don't feel angry you probably don't.

But now I know what is possible to do, anyway. You should attack his weakest points which are his eyes, his throat, his testicles, and his knees. And he can never hold all your body parts at the same time, so you always have one or several parts free to defend yourself with.

With your fingers you can squeeze, tear, push and pull, with your palms you can slap against his ears or up under his nose – but that can lead to the nasal bone being pushed up into his brain so he dies –, with your hands you can squeeze his testicles or pull a finger out of joint, with your fists you can strike against his throat, with your elbows you can strike against his neck or waist, with your teeth you can bite his penis – but I could never do that –, with your feet and heels you can kick against his testicles and knees, with your forehead or back of your head – depending on where he stands – you can thump against his nose, and your knees you can drive up into his crotch.

And you shouldn't believe that you can't give him serious injuries, because if you press too hard on his eyes he can go blind, and if you strike against his throat the windpipe can swell up so he suffocates, and if you kick his testicles he can become unconscious.

But I didn't do anything. Partly it was because I didn't know what to do, but mainly it was because I didn't feel worth defending.

I have been summoned to trial. The letter states what date and time I should be there, and that I am obliged to come. If I stay away without valid reasons, I can be required to pay fines or be brought to court with help from the police. I must manage, though I feel uncertain and would rather avoid it.

Why can't I feel that he didn't have the right to do what he did? I know it and I think it, but I can't feel it. If you don't know what true love is, you may not have the ability to decide what hate is either? If I could feel worthy of love maybe it would be easier? But I can't feel it, because I don't know what it is like. I have never seen it or never got it, so how could I know how it feels? I don't even know if I could receive it if a guy loved me and wanted to show it physically. If a guy wanted to have sex with me out of love and not out of *contempt*, or whatever it is Bernt has felt sometimes when he has slept with me.

I have gone along with so much I haven't liked, and that has made me start despising myself as well and made me unable to react when others have despised me. I don't think I am worth better because I didn't get better from the beginning. I got nothing from mamma and nothing from papa that made me feel loved and valuable. I don't know what I am worth. I may not deserve better than to be despised, maltreated, and raped. Well, I do, but neither that that guy threatened me, hit me, or raped me, makes me hate him. It is as if I don't understand what it means. I didn't think what he did was worse than a visit to the dentist or anything else that is a little unpleasant and painful. You are stiff and tense and just lie there and wait for it to be over… The physical discomfort was the only thing I reacted to.

Bernt and I are not going to be together anymore. He has asked me to move, and I will do it as soon as possible. We have been together for six years and lived together for two. We met when I was sixteen and he was twenty. But now it's over. If he hadn't ended it, I would have done it. It's fine that we agree and don't fight. I hope I am off before the trial has taken place. I haven't told him about the summons, and I don't intend to do it either.

PART FOUR

It's autumn again. From my window I have a view of a small park, and the leaves on the trees and the bushes have begun to turn yellow. It was at this time last year it happened.

It's grandpa's apartment I live in now. It has been empty since he was admitted to the long-term care, and he may never return. I have put most of his furniture and things in the basement storage and brought my own here. I didn't want to move back to mamma.

The apartment is located on Fyrislundsgatan on the third floor. It's a condominium, and I feel safe here. I told the police I was afraid when that guy threatened me, but that wasn't true. I wasn't afraid when it happened, and I haven't been afterwards either.

It's nice to live alone. It's nice to be in peace. I am glad that Bernt threw me out. But I get so gloomy and unenterprising when no one pushes me. I barely get out of bed sometimes when I am free. I lie and listen to sounds from the neighbours. How people flush the toilet, play music, close doors, and go up and down the stairs. But the guy who lives below me I would rather not hear, because he has such a bad taste in music. And preferably you want it to be quiet.

I couldn't stand Bernt in the end. Not even when he started to become more as usual again, could I stand him. I reacted to him like to an annoying fly that buzzed around and didn't leave me alone. I wanted him to be quiet and not come and disturb me with unimportant things that I wasn't interested in. I was nasty and snapped at him, and even though I knew I was unfair and did wrong, I couldn't help it. Finally, he said that he didn't want me there anymore.

I have no friends. Since Petra moved to her boyfriend in Germany, I have only had Bernt, and he is no friend.

This is probably what I have always been afraid of. To live alone and manage myself. But you must make it. And it was good that I realized how wrong my and Bernt's relationship was and that he helped me to put an end to it.

Sometimes I think that love exists, but for the most part I doubt it. What I thought about Göran before was so stupid. He doesn't care about me that way. He still gives me a lift if we leave work at the same time, even though I live in Årsta now. It's as close to his apartment as before but in the opposite direction. Sometimes I have thought about asking him if he wants to come in with me and see how I live, but I don't know what the point would be.

He has a tape in his car that he plays sometimes when we go, and always when I hear it – or a special song on it – I get ready to cry. The music makes me feel like love exists and that he loves me. It's so silly. Why do I think like that when it isn't like that? It's a tape with Arne Lamberth who plays the trumpet, and the song is called Russian Folk Song. I can hardly bear hearing it, but still I have bought a similar tape myself. It's when I lie and listen to it that I can get the idea that I am in love with Göran and he with me.

But that's not the case, and therefore I show almost indifference to him instead. I don't want him to feel sorry for me and wish to comfort me as he did before, just because he knows what I have been through. I want him to be interested in me in any case, but he isn't, and therefore it's better that I don't open at all. But if he isn't interested *now*, he wouldn't have had to be it before either. I don't understand why he wanted to know how I was. That was strange. And how should I interpret that he came to my home when I was sick? What did he mean and want by that?

Now it's done. Now the trial is over. I took a day off, because I didn't want to tell at work what I was to do. I didn't say anything to Göran either, although he knows.

Yes, and so I went there… First, I had to wait in a room outside the courtroom, and there were several other girls that that guy had also raped or tried to rape. Nobody said it, but I understood it from the circumstances. Everyone had company with them except me.

We were called in one by one, and at last it was my turn. I had to sit on a bench to the left in the courtroom, and on the right side sat that guy with his lawyer. There was a man sitting next to me also, but I don't know who he was. Yes, he must have been the prosecutor. And right in front of us sat the lay assessors and the chairman of the court.

I was supposed to tell in my own words what had happened, but it didn't go well, so I was also asked questions, so that I could get through it.

– How were you dressed this evening?

*– I wore a short-sleeved sweater, a long cardigan, long
trousers, and a thin jacket – like a coat – and walking-
shoes.*

– No headgear?

– No.

– But underwear of course?

– Yes, bra and briefs.

*– And some of these garments were taken off from you
by the defendant at the time in question?*

– Yes.

– Can you specify which ones?

– The coat, the long trousers, and the briefs.

– Can you tell me how it happened.

– …

– For example, how did you lose your coat?

– He unbuttoned it and then I ran out of it.

– He unbuttoned your coat?

– Yes.

– Did it happen with your consent, or did you protest?

– I didn't want him to do it, but I didn't say anything.

– You didn't? And you didn't try to stop him?

– No.

– How come?

– I don't know. I couldn't make up my mind to do it.

– You couldn't make up your mind to do it.

– He said he was sexually aroused?

– Yes.

– And what did you do?

– Nothing.

– But then you could no longer have doubts about what his intentions were?

– You let him unbutton your coat, bare your breasts, and pull off your trousers without protesting?
– No, he didn't pull off…
– Is it true that you let this happen without offering any significant resistance?
– Yes.

Now I know what the guy's name is and how old he is. I will try to forget it again. Calling him by name is the same as confirming him, and I can't bring myself to do that. He isn't a real person to me and he will never be either.

I didn't feel anything special when I saw him. To me, he was just the one I pointed out to the police and not the one who raped me. I didn't want to look at him. But I listened to what he said.

He remembered almost nothing at all of what happened that night. He didn't even recognize me, he said. And when asked what he had done earlier in the day, he said that he had hung out in town and drunk beer, and later he had gone with some friends in a car where he had also been drinking, and in the evening he had accompanied another guy home and shared a bottle of strong spirits with him. If he had drunk as much as he said, he should have been quite drunk when he stood there at the street corner and smoked, but it wasn't noticeable.

Or did he lie about it to be able to blame it on that he was so drunk that he didn't know what he was doing when he attacked me? He was asked if he had been standing there waiting for a woman to show up, but he hadn't, he said. He denied that it was planned. But I think it was, because why else would he have stood there? And he only remembered that he had stopped me and asked what time it was and that he had brought me into the yard. Nothing about him having a gun or what else he had done. He had a faint memory of us lying on the ground, but after that he only knew that he had jumped on a bus and gone home. He lived with his mother in Gränby, and when he came home she was up, and she had noticed that he was somehow different and asked what had happened, but he had only said he was tired and gone to bed.

And it was perhaps true that he didn't remember more. I don't know. In any case, it didn't matter because everyone still knew he was guilty. *I* knew it and everyone else as well. And his lawyer didn't seem very positive about him. He sounded more like a prosecutor than a defence counsel when he questioned him.

– How is it, do you have difficulty having normal sexual relationships with women?
   – No, I haven't.
   – You have had normal relationships?
   – Yes, on several occasions.

– Even steady relationships?

– Yes, I was together with a chick for over a year.

– Can you then give an explanation of why you are doing this and assault unknown women?

– Yes, for the most part it depends on the booze. When I'm under the influence of alcohol, it may happen that I'm not fully aware of what I'm doing. I'm getting some kind of blackout.

– You think it's due to the alcohol that you commit sex crimes?

– Yes, for the most part it is. In a sober state, I would never harass anyone.

– You wouldn't? But shouldn't you try to refrain from drinking in that case, given the consequences it may have?

– Yes, but it's not so damn easy to just quit either.

– Thank you, then I have no further questions.

Then it was no more, and I had to go home. It was rather disappointing, because it had gone so fast, and you could tell by the judge's and the prosecutor's manners that it was just a boring job that was to be done.

But it's good that it's over. What he was sentenced to you didn't get to know at the time, but it will come later. I must find out for myself in that case because it's not announced. The minimum sentence for rape is two years, so he probably doesn't get less than that. But I don't care what he is sentenced to. It doesn't interest me. I am not go-

ing to find out. I want the rope to break now, so that
I will be free.

Why can't I stop thinking about it? It doesn't help that the trial is over. I still can't put it behind me. During the trial, it wasn't described in as much detail as during the police interrogations, but it reminded me, and now I have started to dwell on it again.

I had been to the cinema and was on my way to the bus when I met him. While walking, I was thinking about the film I had seen and that I didn't want to go home. That I didn't stop at Stora torget and waited for the bus was due to that. I thought I could walk and spin out the time a bit. It was mostly a feeling and no real thoughts, but I didn't dare tell the police that I had felt that way and that's why I didn't stop on the square.

– So, you had been to the cinema?

– Yes.

– In which cinema?

– Spegeln.

– Spegeln? But then the bus stop on Drottninggatan or Stora torget must be nearer at hand?

– Yes, but I just missed a bus, and I thought I could walk a bit while I waited for the next one and get on at some stop further ahead.

– I understand.

I lied to the police and said that I had missed the bus and that's why I started walking.

I was walking on Vaksalagatan, and when I got to Storgatan I saw a guy standing there at the corner by the electricity store. Yes, and when I had passed him, I heard steps behind me and a voice that said:

"Wait a minute!"

I stopped and turned around, and he came up to me and asked what time it was.

"It's half past ten," I said, and started walking again.

And he followed. He began to walk next to me. At first, he was quiet, but when I just went on without taking any notice of him, he said:

"You don't have to be in such a hurry, do you? Stop and chat for a while."

But I didn't want that, and I said so. That's when he got angry and grabbed my arm.

"I want to chat with you!" he said.

And he pushed me into the gateway between the house walls. I was so surprised that I couldn't make up my mind to offer resistance at first. Then I tried to push past him and out again, but he got in the way and stopped me. There was a two-part iron gate there, and I grabbed it and held on to it, because then I began to realize that he might not let me go. That's when he put his hand in his jacket pocket and pushed the cloth towards me.

"I have a pistol!" he said.

"I don't believe you," I said.

That I said and felt that way, I didn't tell the police either. The normal is to get scared if you are threatened with a weapon. But I didn't believe him and just thought he was ridiculous.

Then he tore me loose from the gate and pushed me into the yard.

– Do you remember if he said anything in connection with him doing this?

   – Yes. "We're going in here!" he said.

   – And what did you answer?

   – I said that I didn't want to.

   – Mhm.

   – Yes, and then I asked what he was doing.

   – Can you repeat what was said word for word as accurately as possible.

   – Yes, first he said that we were going in there, and I said: "Why?" "Because I say so!" he said. Then I asked why he… "Why are you doing this?" I said, and then he said he was…

   – Yes?

   – "I'm horny!" he said.

Inside the gate there was a lamp shining, but further in between the house walls it was dark. It wasn't lit in any windows, because there are old, uninhabited houses around that yard. No one could see us, and no one would hear if I screamed, if I would have to scream.

But I didn't believe it would get worse. When he realized that I didn't want to, he would stop and let me go, I thought. I was so stupid.

And I didn't get loose. He pushed me in where it was dark and pressed me against a wall and unbuttoned my coat. With one hand he held me and with the other he unbuttoned my coat.

– And then? What happened next?

– He started rubbing against me. He rubbed against me with his… lower body.

– Mm. And then?

– He pulled up my sweater and took out a breast and bent down and kissed it.

– How did he do it when he brought it up?

– He lifted it out of the cup on the bra and out over the edge, so to say.

– Mm. And then he bent down and kissed it?

– Yes.

And I just stood there and let him carry on. But when he tried to unbutton my trousers, I offered resistance. I crossed my legs and tried to tear away his hand. When I couldn't remove it, I thought I had to call for help. At the same time, I was afraid he would get angry, so I just *said* I would do it.

"If you don't let go, I'll scream," I said.

I didn't mention that to the police either, because it seemed so ridiculous that I tried to threaten him with it instead of just doing it.

And he didn't care. He opened his fly and took it out. I hadn't believed he would do that. I had believed he would let me go when he had understood that I didn't want to.

But he took it out and wanted it to go in. He tried to pry my legs apart with his hands. When he did that, I got angry and screamed. I knew that no one would come and help me, but I thought he might believe so and get scared and run away.

Instead, he got angry and hit me in my face.

– Did he strike with an open hand or a clenched fist?

– With an open, like a box on the ear.

– How many times?

– Once.

– Was it a hard blow?

– Yes.

– "Now you shut up!" he said. "If you shout again, I'll kill you!" And then he grabbed hold of my neck and banged my head against the wall.

– Was it a heavy thump that caused pain?

– Yes, I got a bump there.

– But he didn't thump so hard that there was a risk that you would lose consciousness?

– No, but I was afraid he would do it again and do it

harder next time.

I didn't think he would kill me, but if he knocked me unconscious, I wouldn't be able to defend myself, so I thought it was best to be quiet. It felt silly to be so close to the street and the sidewalk, where people perhaps came walking, and just let it happen.

And he kept trying to get my trousers off. After a while, I thought he might let me be if he had an ejaculation and suggested that I could jerk him off.

"Yes, do it then, damn it!" he said.

And I tried, but he had almost no erection, and I couldn't make him come. Maybe I did it the wrong way. And I thought: Why does he do this when he isn't even sexually aroused? He had said that he was horny, but he had no erection, and if that had been the case, he would have had that, wouldn't he? I couldn't give it to him either, and when nothing happened I stopped. He didn't get an erection, and I didn't think he would come no matter how long I carried on. So, I stopped.

After that he tore off my briefs. And I don't know, but I thought he might have been a little aroused by what I had done anyway, and that's why he kept on. I had thought he would come, so that he would calm down, but it turned out the other way around.

And I tried to frighten him.

"If I scream again, people will come here and

you will get caught," I said.

I didn't tell the police that I said that. Then he put a hand over my mouth and pressed hard, so I hit my head against the wall again. I felt the smell of nicotine on his fingers, and his hand was so disgusting.

"You know what I said!" he said.

And I hadn't intended to scream again, because I didn't dare, but he couldn't know that. I just wanted him to stop.

But he kept on trying to get it in.

– He tried to insert his penis into the vagina?
– Yes, but it didn't work, because I crossed my legs. And it was too soft and bent.
– He didn't have a strong enough erection?
– No, it was completely slack.

Maybe he wanted to fuck me with a slack cock as a punishment, I was almost about to say during the interrogation, like a little joke. And I thought it might seem like I was disappointed that it was slack.

Why am I so crazy? It creeps inside me with discomfort when I think of all the weird thoughts and ideas I can get.

He didn't give up, but it didn't work, and in the end, he became angry and tore me away from the wall and threw me to the ground. But I got up again and started running. He grabbed my coat, but I ran out of it and away towards the gate.

I thought it ended there, but it didn't. He got hold of me again. When I had slipped out of my coat, he grabbed me again and threw me to the ground and sat on me.

– And then?

– Then he moved up and tried to get… tried to push it into my mouth. But I didn't open my mouth, and it was completely soft and flabby, so it didn't work.

– He tried to force his penis into your mouth?

– Yes, but I didn't open it.

– And how did he react to that?

– He said that if I didn't open it, he would kill me.

– He threatened to kill you?

– Yes. But I still couldn't. I thought I would…

– Take it easy. There is no hurry.

– No, I…

– So, you refused to take his penis in your mouth?

– Yes.

– And what did he do then?

– Said he would kill me.

– Did he show any signs in his behaviour that he was prepared to resort to more serious violence in order to get his will?

– Yes, he was angry.

– How did his anger manifest itself?

– He swore. But then he started pulling it instead and rubbing it against my cheeks.

– He rubbed his penis against your face?

– Yes, pressed and rubbed. And finally, he got… an erection and tried again, but I…

– Mm?

– I didn't open my mouth, and he grabbed my hair so I couldn't turn my face away and pressed against my lips. "Suck, God damnit!" he said. But I couldn't, and he… I tried to get loose, and he got even angrier and raised himself a little and tore up my cardigan and forced his way down between my legs. I couldn't stop him. And he…

– Yes?

– He got it in and started…

– He inserted his penis into the vagina?

– Yes, and started…

– …doing intercourse movements?

– Yes.

– Can you tell me what you were thinking while it was going on? While he was inside…

– Yes, I thought it was fortunate that I was taking birth control pills and that it was strange that he dared to do it so close to the street where people passed by. It wasn't even dark where we lay, because I had run away a bit before he got hold of me again. And I thought – or felt – that it hurt when I was rubbed against the gravel.

– Yes, you… But you didn't think of calling for help?

– No, I didn't dare.

– How long do you estimate that the intercourse itself lasted?

– I don't know. But it seemed that he couldn't.

– That he was unable?

– Yes, to get…

– …an ejaculation?

– Yes.

– What was it that gave you that impression?

– That he got annoyed and exerted himself, so he became sweaty. And I thought that if he didn't come, he might get even angrier and take the anger out on me and kill me.

– You felt threatened with death?

– No, but I thought it could go that way if he didn't get an ejaculation. So, I was hoping he would get it. I'm taking birth control pills, so it wouldn't have… But he stopped before he was done.

– He didn't ejaculate?

– What…

– He interrupted before ejaculating?

– Yes.

– And how did you notice that it was that way?

– Because nothing ran out when I got up.

– Mm… He interrupted, you say.

– Yes, suddenly he just jumped up and ran away.

– Did you see in which direction he ran?

– Yes, further in.

– Further into the yard?

– Yes.

– He didn't take the same way as you had come then, through the gateway out towards Vaksalagatan?

– No.

– And what did you do?

– I sat up. At first, I lay on the ground for a while, and

then I know I got up, but I don't remember going out on the street. I don't know how I got there.

— You have a gap in your memory there?

— Yes.

— But you remember the rest? That you met that guy who helped you into Lucullus and…

— Yes.

Lying underneath him on the ground with my legs heavily pressed apart by his body, pressed against the gravel
by his weight, my face turned to the side, my chin to my
shoulder, my arms locked by his hands
cannot get loose
Hear his hissing breath, feel how he bumps, pant, moans,
bumps
take birth control pills, do not risk getting pregnant
Slide backwards for each impact, roll on the stones,
scrape against the gravel, rub against the ground for
each impact
it hurts
Feel his hands squeezing my wrists, holding my wrists
tightly and pressing my arms to the ground
strange that he dares to do it so close to the street where
people might pass by
Hear the air hiss in, out, in, out, through his mouth
Feeling his alcohol-scented breath against my face, keep-
ing my head aside, pressing my chin against my shoulder
do not want to feel
Trying to twist my body and get away, trying to get

loose
cannot beat him
Shut my eyes
do not want to feel, do not feel

Open my eyes and see his face, see his tense, sweaty face
he is ugly
Twitch and get my arms free, throw my upper body to
the side, get thrown back to the ground, hitting my head
against the ground, feeling sick, feeling queasy
must not vomit
See his parted lips and half-open mouth
he is disgusting
Close my eyes and lie still

Do not know more, do not know more until he swears
and jumps up, is up, stands up and breathes heavily
he is done, when was he done
Look at his hand, stare at his hand, stare at the hand that
puts the penis into the jeans, jerks and tears the zipper,
pulls up the zipper on his fly
See when he turns around and disappears, disappears
into darkness, engulfs by darkness and is gone
is gone

Remain on the ground, lie on my back with the cardigan
slipped up and my legs apart
cannot get up
Feel how the wind cools where his body has been, feel
how it stings and burns between my legs

must get up
Bring my legs together, pull down the cardigan, turn my
upper body to the side, take support with my hands
against the ground, lift myself up, sit

Sit in the gravel, straighten my clothes, brush away dust
and debris that has stuck to the cardigan
he did not take my bag, the bag is over there, must go
and get my bag
Gently change position, slowly struggle up on my feet,
up on my feet

Stand
must pick up the bag and my clothes, must get dressed
and go home, must go home
My legs are trembling, trying to relax, taking a few stag-
gering steps, getting dizzy, breaking out in a cold sweat,
staggering
must not faint, must not fall, must go and
My ears feel blocked up, it whispers in my head, my head
is in a whirl, it turns black

PART FIVE

I have begun to get annoyed at the guy who lives below me because he has the sound of his stereo too loud on when he listens to music. He doesn't play at night, and it's allowed to play before ten o'clock in the evening, but I am disturbed anyway, because I don't want to hear it. I get so angry that I tremble, and my heart starts beating faster, and I get difficulty breathing. I wish I dared to go down and tell him that if he doesn't immediately turn off his fucking noise, I will break both him and his stereo.

But I can't do that. You have no right. And actually, I don't want to do things that can give him a possibility to put me away. The only thing that probably would work is to ask him. But I can't ask him. I don't like him. He is the type who likes to walk around stripped to the waist and show off and who thinks he is strong and good-looking and smart even though he actually is exactly the opposite.

Once when I was on my way down, he came out into the stairwell with a beer can in his hand and was wearing only tight jeans and an ugly necklace, and when I walked past him, he stared at me and said hello. I didn't answer, because I don't want to deal with idiots.

But I must as long as he disturbs. Every time he turns on music, there is a twinge in my stomach, and I can't relax and continue with what I was doing until it's quiet again. I become paralyzed and can't do what I want as long as it lasts.

And I can never feel sure it won't start again any minute. I am on my guard all the time and just wait for it to come. He trespasses when he forces me to listen to sounds that I don't want to hear. But what should I do? I have no right to ask him to stop.

And I don't want to talk to him. But I can't just let it be either. I have pounded on the floor a few times, but either he hasn't heard, or he doesn't care. And I have been thinking about writing a note and putting it in his mailbox. But I don't think it should be needed, because if you are normal you understand that you disturb others if you play music as loud as he does. He should understand it himself, but he apparently doesn't, and therefore I don't want to deal with him. I don't want to deal with a person who is that stupid and ruthless and only thinks about his own needs.

At the same time, I think I might be overreacting because I am reminded of something else I have been forced to, and if it weren't for that, I wouldn't care so much about what he does. I don't know. I don't know if I am right or wrong. I dare not trust what I feel. I *think* you should have the right not to be disturbed, but you don't get support for it even in the law, so I don't know.

Last night I dreamed that I was wandering about in a big hospital looking for a phone. I knew it was important that I found one so I could call, but there was no one to ask, because everyone was busy, and I had to search myself. I hurried back and forth through long corridors, in and out of rooms, up and down stairs, and there were people everywhere, but no one seemed to see me or care about me.

Göran doesn't seem interested in me any longer. Apparently, it was just that he thought that Bernt was abusing me that worried him. Or couldn't he handle me telling him about the attempted rape?

He still doesn't know that it was a completed rape. I haven't told him. I thought he maybe would ask a little about what had happened right after I had showed him the newspaper clipping, but he didn't, and that made me unsure. That's probably why I haven't told him. That he didn't ask may also be due to me, that I have withdrawn and almost taken up an indifferent attitude towards him so that I won't imagine things that don't exist. In any case, I understand that it mostly depends on me how it will be, because I actually don't think he is afraid.

Sometimes I think about what it would feel like to sleep with a guy who I wanted to sleep with and not just slept with because I thought I had to, and then I think of Göran. Not that it would be him, but if I imagine a guy who is like him, who doesn't need to assert himself and show his power, and who I wouldn't feel despised and exploited by, I think I could be open and enjoy it.

I don't know why I get so angry when the guy below turns on music. I think it's because I can't get away and that I am so powerless. I don't want to feel powerless and cowardly. Sometimes I imagine that I push him down the stairs so that he breaks his neck, or cut the tires on his car, or phone him and wake him up in the middle of the night every time he has disturbed, or…

Last time he started playing, I called him. I was so angry that it felt like I would go crazy if I didn't try to stop it. I found the number in the telephone directory by means of the last name on the door and the street address.

"Turn off that fucking noise!" I said when he answered.

"Who's talking?" he said.

Then I hung up.

Now he at least knows what I think. He can't know for sure that I was the one who called, but he should be able to figure it out.

But he didn't turn it off. He might play even more and even higher now, just to take revenge and show his power.

And I knew he wouldn't care. It feels a little better to have done it, because if he continues now that he knows he is disturbing, it proves that I have perceived him correctly. But there is still nothing I can do to stop him. It feels so unfair. Why can he torment and ruin things for me, while I am not even allowed to defend myself against him? How can it be permitted? I don't understand that.

The only thing I can do is to hate and despise him, and now that I no longer have to doubt that I have a reason for it, I might be able to ignore what he is doing and look down on him instead of getting angry. I will at least try, because I can't go on working myself up all the time. I don't want him to succeed in making me angry. I don't want to deal with him. He is a disgusting little piece of shit who isn't even worth spitting on. I don't deal with idiots like him. It's under my dignity to notice him. He doesn't exist, and therefor he *can't* upset me.

Now when I know what can happen at home, and I am sitting with Göran in his car, it feels like it did when I had been driven home by the police and I didn't want to go in to Bernt. I would rather stay with Göran or come in with him. But he has never invited me. He perhaps believes that I don't want to. He may have felt rejected when he has hugged me and tried to comfort me and I both times just have stood there stiff as a poker and not showing any response.

I dare not open to him. I don't know what he feels, and I am afraid I will misunderstand. But I look forward to the car ride with him every day. If he leaves work before me or stays longer, so I have to take the bus, I am disappointed.

We say almost nothing while we drive. Just a little about work sometimes and about other unimportant things. Never about ourselves. He gives me space, and I don't know what to fill it with. He doesn't fill his either. We are both equally quiet and withdrawn.

Sometimes when I wake up in the middle of the night and it's completely quiet everywhere, I think that silence is love. And in a book, I read: "Integrity (right) – the right of every human being to have her individuality and inner sphere respected and not to be subjected to disturbing interference."

That's how I feel that Göran is towards me, and that's why I can imagine that he is in love with me. But all that is positive isn't love. I get that. And as soon as I think I am in love with him, I feel like an immature teenager who is secretly in love with a teacher who isn't interested back. He is only five years older than me, so it can't be the age difference that makes me feel childish compared to him sometimes, and it's not because he looks down on me and treats me condescendingly, because he doesn't.

I don't know what it's due to. All I know is that love is too big for me. Perhaps we could have sex, but not love.

When I got home from work, the guy who lives below me was out in the parking lot by his car, and when I passed, he called out after me. At first, I thought I would pretend that I didn't hear and just go in, because I didn't want to talk with him, but then it felt like I had to do it anyway, to give him a chance to show that he… No, I don't know what I was thinking. But I turned and went up to him, and he stretched out his hand and said:

"Hi! I don't think I have introduced myself. My name is Tomas, and I live in the apartment below you."

And I took his hand and said my name although I didn't want to do that either. Why is it so hard not to be polite? And he said:

"I think you have complaints about me?"

"Have I?" I said, because I didn't intend to admit more than he could prove.

"Yes, I have asked all the neighbours, and no one has had anything to object to me playing my music, so it must be you. But I think it's better to discuss things and try to agree, and I just want to point out that I have every right to play, as long as I don't do it at night."

"Good for you then!" I said, thinking he was so disgusting and ugly that I could hardly look at him.

"However, as you may know, shaking rugs from the balcony isn't allowed," he said.

And I may have shaken some rugs sometimes, but I said nothing, and he stared at me and continued:

"So, if you don't stop doing it, I'll talk to the association."

"Yes, just go ahead!" I said.

He made me feel at a disadvantage, because I knew that I had done wrong while he hadn't done anything at all that was against the regulations.

"Are we agreed then?" he said.

"No, we are not!" I said and left.

Afterwards, I felt completely annihilated. It felt like I could just as well lie down and die. Because he had managed to turn everything around. He can continue to disturb, while I am not even allowed to shake a small rug from my balcony. It's so unfair. And for the most part, I haven't *shaken* the rugs but only had some hanging over the balcony parapet while I have been cleaning. But I am glad if dust has fallen down on his balcony!

I feel cheated. Why did I walk up to him and talk to him though I didn't want to? And now he probably hates me. I almost dare not go down the stairs and past his door in case he should show up. I don't feel safe at home anymore. That's not how it should be, is it? You shouldn't have to go around and be scared in your own home.

But I am. I don't know where to go to be sure nothing will happen. And when he starts playing, I can't get away. I must put up with it until he pleases to stop. I don't want it to be that way, but what should I do? There is no help to be had.

Maybe it's just as well that I move. But why should I who is right leave, while he who is wrong can stay? I can't do that either. I can't give in to him.

I am not physically afraid of him. I am not afraid he is going to attack me by force. If he does, I report him to the police. I almost wish he would do it, so I can put him away.

What I am afraid of is that I will be fooled. I am afraid I will lose the sense of how much I hate and despise him, so I let him reach me again.

Due to a newspaper article that Viola was reading at the coffee table at work, the conversation got on to rape, and then Egon came out with that all women fantasize about being raped.

I felt that Göran was looking at me, as if to see my reaction, but I don't care what Egon says, because I already know he is stupid and looks down on women.

"In your dreams, man," said Viola, who doesn't like Egon's style either. "And when it comes to rapists, I think they should be castrated!"

Why don't I feel the same way as she does? Why don't I hate the guy in town for what he did to me? Why don't I react like everybody else? Why am I so weird?

But the guy who lives below I hate. I shouldn't have walked up to him and talked to him when he called out to me, because it made me unsure again. It made me feel like I didn't know what to do if he did it again, or if he phoned me or came up.

But now I know. If he shouted, I would pretend not to hear, if he called, I would put the receiver down, and if he came up, I would slam the door. At first, I thought I couldn't be so impolite and that it would just make him even angrier. I felt scared, but not because he is big and strong, but because he is so insensitive and stupid that you are doomed to lose against him. I thought I had to answer when he addressed me, just as I thought I had to answer what time it was when the guy in town came and asked me about it.

You are just taken in. I am not going to listen to the guy below and feel hated. I am going to listen to myself and hate *him*, because then I don't know and don't care about what he feels. Then I don't need to be afraid. It's so disgusting to think of that I let him take my hand. Why did I do that?

It feels like I could kill him. I want to get back at him and get rid of him once and for all. I want to force him to confess and regret and be frightened and ask for mercy, and when he has done that, I will kick him and torment him and finally kill him, for it's he or I, and I want it to be me, for I am right and he is wrong.

But that's not how it will be. I can't put an end to it as long as he stays. But if I had a gun I would shoot him, and I wouldn't care if I ended up in prison, because as it is now I am already in prison, and it would at least feel like a relief to have killed him and know that he no longer existed.

Bernt has been here. We have neither met nor talked on the phone since he helped me move, but last night he came here and rang the doorbell. When I opened, he said it was something he wanted to talk to me about and asked if he could come in for a while. I didn't actually want to let him in, because he was standing there with a cigarette, and he wasn't quite sober either, I noticed. But I didn't think I could just slam the door right in his face either without finding out what he wanted. Why do I never learn?

What he wanted was to lay me, and when I rejected him, he got angry.

– Ah, don't be grumpy now. I like you Susanne, and I want to show it.

– Yes, but not like this.

– Yes, come on now.

– No, I don't want to.

– Sure as hell you want to.

– No, I say.

– For the sake of old love?

– Love?

– Yes, come on!

– No! You hear what I say!

– Yes, you say one thing and mean another.

– I don't at all!

– Yes, I know you, Susanne. I know you damn well, and I know what you need.

– No, you don't.

– But now you don't have anyone to fuck with either, do you? Or?

– It doesn't concern you in that case! And let me go now!

– No, I won't let you go until you have admitted.

– Admitted what?

– That you need cock.

– Let go, I said!

– Don't be awkward!

– Stop now!

– But this is how you want it. Right? You like rough stuff.

– No, I don't!

– Yes, you like to be raped.

He held me and pushed me down on the bed. At last I got so angry that I felt like hitting him. But I didn't have time to do it before he threw me away and left.

When he was gone, I cried. *You fucking idiot! I thought. Why do you have to be so stupid? I'll never let you in again!* I imagined that he was trying to get on top of me and that I pulled my legs up and put my feet against his stomach and kicked him back as hard as I could. I felt that I needed to get him away from me. I lay on my back in bed and did it in reality several times, even though he wasn't there. I did what I should have done from the beginning. Because the truth is that I have never wanted to have sex with him, and I have never wanted *him*. I don't understand how I could once believe that I loved him and that he loved me.

Last night I dreamed that there was a burglary in my apartment. When I got home, everything was broken and destroyed. And the burglar was still there. He saw me coming, but he didn't care, but just kept knocking on the furniture. I shouted that I should report him to the police and claim damages for everything that was destroyed, and I said that what he did felt worse than being stabbed.

Then I woke up. In my dream, I felt so powerless when I noticed that he didn't care about how I felt and I realized that I would never be able to make him understand it either.

That's the way it is in reality as well. I don't know what to do to make it good. There is nothing to do.

At first it didn't feel like this at all. At that time, I almost thought that what had happened was exciting and interesting. But now I understand that no matter what you have been through, and no matter how you manage, there is no reason to feel remarkable. Nobody cares about it anyway. No one cares about it and no one can help you.

I want the guy below to die. I want to torment

and torture him as he torments and tortures me, because I can't stand feeling powerless and hate every day. I will take his fucking cock and lay it on a cutting board while it's still a part of him and cut it lengthwise. He should be conscious the entire time and feel everything. Then I will chop it into small pieces and run the pieces down his throat one by one, and when he lies there ready to suffocate, I will laugh and ask if there is anything else he wants to point out before he dies. Because he is going to die. All of his kind must die, so that I won't have to see their disgusting bodies and faces and won't have to hear their false voices and words. I will kill them all, because not a single one of them has the right to live.

Why didn't I defend myself against the guy in town? Why did I let him do what he did? Yes, I know why, but it feels so incomprehensible now that I just let it happen. I am ashamed I was so passive. I understand if the police officers thought I was reacting strangely.

It would never have had to happen. I know I could have escaped if I had just got angry. It was that I didn't get angry, and not that I was scared, that made me passive. I wasn't afraid he would kill me. I didn't believe he would. But I didn't want to be beaten, and I thought that what he did wasn't so bad. Not from the beginning anyway.

Then I don't know. All I know is that I should have defended myself as soon as he turned up, so that it had never happened. As long as we were out on the street, he didn't have a chance. He didn't. He would never have managed to get me with him if I had reacted normally. I hadn't needed to know any grips or tricks to get away. I would have succeeded anyway, if I had only been able to feel what I wanted and didn't want. I must blame myself for being raped. Because I was an easy victim who didn't have sense enough to offer resistance. I followed him almost voluntarily into that yard. I only defended myself half-heartedly. I know I did. But I hadn't needed to be so compliant and stupid.

Yesterday evening, when I went out with the garbage, the guy below suddenly appeared on the
stairs. I wasn't prepared to meet him and felt completely bewildered. I just stood there and let him
talk. I didn't leave as I had decided to do.

"Your flower boxes are a problem for me," he
said. "Water drips from them down on my balcony,
and they attract insects that bother me when I sit
there and sun."

Is he sunning on the balcony in October? It was
just bullshit. And what does he think his stinking
cigarettes do, when I want to sit on *my* balcony? But
I said nothing, and he stared at me and continued:

"I hope you fix it!"

I didn't get a word out, and I am glad about that
now, because I don't want to give him even a little
word.

"Are we agreed then?" he said.

Then I went in and closed the door.

And at first, I didn't feel anything, except that I
was glad that I hadn't given him an answer. But I
shouldn't have stayed there and listened to him

either. I should have understood that he was just trying to get at me and left at once.

He can go to hell! He would just dare to speak to me again! He has no right to it. A word from him is an abuse as great as if he were trying to rape me. No, it's worse, because a physical attack you can't misinterpret and have the right to defend yourself against, but when hatred is hidden and wrapped in ordinary words, you become unsure and don't know what to do. And I don't think he deserves to know how I feel. Getting mad at him and showing it to him would be the same as confirming his existence and significance, and that's the last thing I want to do. I don't want anything to do with him at all. When he came up the stairs I would have reacted as if I neither saw nor heard him and went in as soon as I had thrown the garbage bag away.

Later I began to think about Bernt and how he was, and I thought he did the same to me as the guy below does. I became sad when I remembered that he didn't care about me and that he tried to get at me just because I was me.

Because that's what he did. As long as I didn't show what I felt nothing happened. Then he was satisfied. But as soon as I was honest and tried to say no, he got angry. He couldn't admit the truth, and therefore he needed to try to depress me and take revenge on me when I questioned the lie.

I didn't know I was sorry for what he did. When it happened, I felt almost nothing. But when I think about it now, I feel like I can't forgive him because he attacked me when I was at my weakest and needed help and comfort. Why did he do that? What was it that made him feel so threatened? What he did was almost worse than what the guy in town did. Because Bernt knew me and was supposed to love me.

Maybe it was because the guy reminded me of Bernt that I wasn't negative enough from the beginning? Maybe he felt familiar to me, even though I didn't know who he was? Maybe it was because he had the same kind of charisma that Bernt used to have sometimes, that I didn't have sense enough to be afraid of him?

When Bernt had sex with me, I could never enjoy it. You can't be open to a person you don't trust. He wasn't open to me either. I didn't love him, and he didn't love me. We each just played a role. I was a sexual object to him, and he was a father, who was always there and never disappeared, to me. That's what I needed at that time. That's why it felt like he loved me. But it wasn't love. We never quarrelled, and we agreed on everything, because we never showed each other who we really were. It was part of the agreement that we shouldn't do that. To leave the role and be honest was to break the agreement.

And I did. I withdrew without caring that he wasn't prepared for it and couldn't handle it. Even before the rape I had begun to feel dissatisfied, although I hadn't really admitted it to myself, and afterwards, when he reacted so weirdly, I couldn't wink at it any longer. I think he unknowingly recognized himself in the rapist and that's why he became angry and couldn't care about me. He suspected me of having agreed to what that guy did to me, because I never protested when he himself had sex with me against my will. He couldn't take sides with me, because in that case he would have had to get rid of a part of himself.

It feels like I have been hated and exploited all my life. It was easier before when I didn't really know what I was feeling. But I can't close myself again and shut my eyes to the truth. It's what people do or don't do that shows how it really is. And now… I don't know how it will be. No one can know and understand everything.

When I had gone to bed and was to sleep, I felt that Göran was lying behind me, very close to me, and protected my body with his. It was just a fantasy, but it felt warm and safe, and when he slipped into me, it was so arousing that I had to masturbate to put an end to it.

Afterwards I thought: There is nothing wrong with me. I can feel desire and enjoy. I am not frigid.

Then I cried and fell asleep.

It isn't true that evil should be driven away by evil.

There has been a burglary at work. I was the one who discovered it. First, I saw that the door to the office was open, and then I saw that the drawers in several of the desks were pulled out and that things were scattered all over the floor. My legs were shaky, and I felt almost sick, but I walked around and looked in every room to see what it looked like. In the adjoining room, a wall cabinet was broken, and things were torn out, but otherwise there wasn't anything.

Yes, and Egon came, and I showed him what had happened, and he called the police. Only a radio and the money in the coffee box were missing, but it should still be reported.

When the police arrived, Göran and Viola were also there. The police officers talked to Egon and examined the cupboard and the door to the office and the drawers in the desks that had been opened. The front door had also been broken, but I hadn't noticed because it was shut and had locked itself again.

I thought it was strange that the policemen only

talked to Egon and not to me since it was I who had discovered the burglary. I was disappointed and felt ignored when no one turned to me. I wanted the police to be interested in me again, even though it wasn't about me now. I know it isn't normal to feel that way, and I am ashamed when I think about how strange I react sometimes, but at least no one but myself knows about it. No one will ever know either, because that's the most shameful and forbidden secret I have.

When the policemen had left, I felt dejected. At first, I didn't understand what it was, but then I began to think about the crime scene investigation that was done on the yard after the rape. I thought about people coming there and collecting my clothes and putting my torn briefs in a bag which later ended up in an office with the police and was thrown in a waste-paper basket when I was there to fetch my clothes. And I thought about the coat and the trousers that I couldn't use anymore and had to throw away so as not to be reminded. I kept the cardigan and the shoes, but the rest I got rid of.

When I got home, mamma called. I compelled myself to listen to what she had to say and decided I wouldn't interrupt her but let her carry on until she ended the conversation herself. I thought I would endure it without trying to get away. I hadn't eaten and was hungry, but I wanted to test her and see how long it would take before she stopped.

It took twenty-three minutes. For twenty-three minutes she took advantage of me before she was satisfied.

When we had hung up, I thought: *Go to hell fucking rape bitch!*

Then I began to cry and call for mamma.

The guy below has moved. He is the grandson of the old man who owns the apartment and stayed here only temporarily. It was the old man himself who told me when we met outside his door. He said he hoped that "the boy behaved" while he lived here. I didn't have time to answer before he had gone into his apartment. But I hope he will never lend the apartment to his fucking grandson again.

All the men who have treated me badly are gone: Leif Holmkvist, Bernt Gustafsson, Glenn Nyberg, and Tomas Dahlin. Now that I am sure of their guilt, I can express their names, and all of them should be charged and publicly exposed.

What drives a perpetrator to do what he does? I want to know and understand, which is why I have borrowed two books about rape at the library. One is called "Violence against Women" by Eva Ekselius and the other one is called "Men who Rape" by Nicholas Groth.

I have cribbed the most important parts from

each one of them.

Rape can occur anywhere: at home, in a park, in a stair-well, in a car. The woman may even have gone to bed and fallen asleep. There is no place where she goes safe.

Rape is a complicated, contradictory, and difficult act. It is governed by a variety of needs and motives, often unconscious to the perpetrator. It is possible to distinguish certain patterns in the underlying driving forces. There is a strong need to deny sexual anxiety and doubts about one's own masculinity. There is the need to reduce or escape the feeling of weakness, vulnerability, inadequacy. There is the need to replace these feelings with power, control, strength, invulnerability. There is also the need to vent anger, bitterness, disappointment, and hatred towards all women by hurting, insulting, and humiliating one of them.

Men who commit rape do not do so because they are sexually frustrated or because they suffer under the pressure of an extremely strong sexual drive. Rape often has very little to do with sexuality. For most rapists, it satisfies completely different needs. The rape gives rise to feelings of anger and hatred and it satisfies – for a brief moment – his need to feel power and strength.

To the rapist, sexuality is, in fact, somewhat ugly, filthy, dirty. That is why he uses it to offend and humiliate the woman.

The rapist is in fact a person with serious mental disorders that complicates his relationships with other people, and which, when he is in a stressful situation, gets an outlet in a sexual act. His most pronounced mental defect is the absence of any form of intimate emotional relationship with other people, men or women. He finds it difficult to show warmth, trust, compassion, and empathy for the problems of others, and his relationships with other people lack mutuality, he is unable to take and give.

It doesn't help to know and understand.

It's windy outside. Autumn leaves swirl around in the air. The trees and the bushes in the park will soon be black and bare.

What should I do all winter more than work? I have no friends and no special interests. In the evenings I watch TV or read. I drink tea and listen to music and think. That's all I do, apart from all practical things. Bernt is gone, and I don't want to spend time with mamma, and I only meet Göran at work and when he drives me home.

I have told him about the trial and that I wasn't the only victim. I haven't said more, and he hasn't asked. He still believes it was just an attempted rape. It feels better now that I know that not even the guy who did it remembers it properly. That I am alone to remember it and that the rope to him no longer exists.

I understand why Göran doesn't ask. I haven't asked him about the accident with his sister either. It's who you are, and who you have become from what you have been through, that's important, not how things have happened.

I should go out dancing and meet guys again. I should check out which university courses I should apply to for this spring. Even before it happened, I had started thinking about continuing my studies. Sociology or psychology is what I have thought of in the first place. But there are other subjects that can be interesting to study if I wouldn't be accepted for my first-hand choices. I will see how I feel this spring when it's time to apply.

I dreamed that I found an injured cat outside the gate. It was crouching and looked at me with a tormented gaze. I didn't dare to examine it to see how hurt it was, but I couldn't leave it alone either, so I just stood there crying. After a while it got up laboriously and began to walk away, and then I saw that the fur under its stomach was completely soaked with blood. When it noticed that I wasn't going to help it, it went away so as not to bother me anymore.

How long did I lie unconscious in the yard before I woke up? I see my body lying there in the gravel on the ground like a dirty bundle. I must have awoken and got up, but I don't remember it.

Otherwise, I remember all that happened. I remember all the movements, thoughts, and words, and I know how it felt in my body. I have relived what happened both from the outside and from the inside, and I have learned to get angry and speak out and to want to defend myself and dare to go to a counterattack. I know and understand why abuse occurs, and I no longer allow myself to be treated badly by others.

Yet it doesn't disappear. I try to think about the future and feel free, but I just feel shut in and isolated. It's like getting lost in a dark forest and not finding the right way out.

Why am I crying a lot more now than I did in the beginning? The first week I didn't cry at all. Not the second one either. I was so hard and impassive at that time and thought that what had happened wasn't much to care about.

I felt superior to him. Physically he was more than twice as strong as I am, but mentally he felt like a selfish little kid who just wanted to have and took what he could. I didn't think so, but that's how I perceived him. I couldn't feel like a helpless victim of him when I actually looked down on him.

But he hurt me. He beat me and humiliated me and exploited me. He used violence to have his will. Why don't I feel anything when I think about it?

Did I want it to happen? If it hadn't happened, I might never have learned what I know now. And if I hadn't become alone, I might never have been able to concentrate on trying to find out. Bernt was probably right when he felt threatened.

In a book I read: "Victims and perpetrators were playing a game against each other, which led to the crime. Who was guilty and who was innocent was difficult to determine, as they were not familiar with the various ways of playing. The guilt was probably evenly distributed, as the crime couldn't have taken place without the other person's participation."

Was that what happened? Were we two about it? Is that why I can't hate him?

If I believe I have learned things from what happened, I should be happy now, but I am not. It just feels empty. I feel shut in in an empty room and can't get out. It's creeping inside me, like I am about to burst, but no matter how hard I try, I don't know what to do to get the door open.

I will never know. I will never understand. I will never be free.

I am freezing. I have a fever. I am sick. I can't bear to be up. I am lying in bed in the dark waiting for it to pass.
Can you tell me what you were thinking while it was going on

Everything is a mess. Images, voices, words.
What has happened here then

Soon it's Christmas. I am not going to celebrate Christmas this year. It's nothing to celebrate.

It hurts in my ears and in my throat.
He seized you by the throat

What day is it today? It's Saturday. Nobody knows I am sick. It started last night and now it's soon Sunday.
Tell me what he did to you

I am crying.

Didn't you understand that it was intercourse he was after

I am freezing. The quilt and the blankets don't help. Nothing helps.
You didn't think to call for help

I don't have a thermometer and don't know how high my fever is. Once when I was little I had over forty degrees. I may have as high a fever now, as weak and slack as I feel.
Do you mean he had no erection
Mamma put her hand on my forehead.
You're burning hot honey
I am crying.

What is it that thumps?
He thumped your head against the wall
Is it my heart pounding? Is it my heartbeat I hear in my ears?

It's foggy in my head. My thoughts just fly around. Sometimes it feels like I want to scream.
If you shout I'll kill you

Did I fall asleep? It's too hot under the blankets. I am sweating. My hair sticks to my forehead and my neck. It hurts all over my body. My skin is burning. The quilt and the blankets are too heavy. I can't breathe.

Did he squeeze so you had difficulty breathing
Getting overheated like this can't be good. You
might die of it.
You felt threatened with death
I have no antipyretic to take either. Maybe I can
cool myself down with a wet towel on my forehead, like papa did once when he had fallen asleep
in the sun. It feels dangerous to be this hot.
Don't be namby-pamby girl

Is the radio on? Why did I turn on the radio? What
was it I was going to listen to?
How did you interpret his behaviour?
I can't bear hearing. I must get up and turn off the
radio.
You didn't realize the seriousness of the situation
I can't rise. I curl up under the covers.
No, now you must not lie down

My head aches. My whole face aches.
Did he strike with an open or clenched hand

What does my body do? When I lie on my back, my
arms cross under my breasts
And then he bent down and kissed it
and my hands grab the sweater on each side and
hold on.
Can you describe how he held his hands
Sometimes the right hand grabs the left wrist over
my stomach or squeezes my fingers.

Were there two or more fingers he stuck in
My body holds me so that I don't slip into the fever
fog and disappear.
What has happened to you then
I am sad and cry.

It's not the radio that sounds. It's me.
Whining is the worst thing I know
Whining was the worst thing papa knew.

I am awake and sleeping alternately. The hours go
by. When I feel better, I am going to shower and
wash my hair and put on clean underwear and
change the bed sheets.

Voices outside the door. Running steps on the
stairs.
The front door is locked. No one can come in.
We're going in here
It must go in

Why did I let the injured cat down? Why couldn't I
help it?
You like to be raped

He rubbed his penis against your face
He tried to force his penis into your mouth
He inserted his penis into the vagina

Yes, he did.

Yes, he did!

I wail and cry.

I cry because I feel sorry for myself. I cry out of self-pity.

Feeling self-pitying is weak and shameful. Who made me believe that? It was papa who made me believe that. I am glad that he disappeared. He wasn't anything to have. He was wrong.

I feel sorry for myself now that I am alone and lie sick and no one helps me. I feel sorry for myself when I was alone and was raped and no one helped me.

No, it was my own fault.

But if it hadn't been me? If I had seen it happen in a movie? If I had seen him assault her, force her, threaten her, beat her, exploit her, and rape her? Wouldn't I have felt sorry for her in that case and wanted to help her?

Yes, I would.

Yes, I would!

Why didn't I understand?

No, don't do it, I don't want to, please don't do it, let me be, please let me be, why can't you let me be, why do you do this, what have I done, why do I have to when I don't want to, why can't I be spared, I don't want to, why don't you care what I feel, why don't you care that I don't want to, why do you do this, I don't want to, you must not do this, please please don't do it, I don't want

to, you must not do it, don't do it, you have no right to
do it, no no no, oh good God why does this happen, why
does it happen, why does it have to happen, it hurts, it's
disgusting, I feel sick, I can't take it, why is no one helping me, what should I do, why is there nothing I can do,
oh good God why is no one helping me

PART SIX

I get a lift from Göran home.

We listen to music,
and when Russian Folk Song is played, I cry.

I am completely open,
and nothing hinders me from feeling.

I am not trying to hide my tears,
and I feel his silent awareness of me.

I haven't told him, but it feels like he knows anyway.
He knows who I am.
That's the only important thing, not what others
have done to me.

He has been here all along,
and now I am here too.

I am sitting beside him in the dark,
and the clear tones of the trumpet go straight into

me and fill me with sorrow.
I hear tenderness, sadness, consideration and consolation and a rising cry of pain and triumph,
and I feel that love exists.

This is how it ends, and this is how it begins,
and that is all I know.